"He is amongst us!"

Merry Christmas!

A

Ragamuffin
Christmas

An Advent Journey

Craig Daliessio

Published by The Morgan Group

Copyright 2010 by The Morgan Group

Printed in the
United States of America

Brennan Manning is quoted from:
"The Relentless Tenderness of Jesus" Pg 205
Copyright 1996, 2004 by Brennan Manning
Published by Revell division of Baker Books
PO Box 6287 Grand Rapids MI 49516

A Word Before

What folks are saying...

"Craig's book is an account of a man's pilgrimage to faith - through parenting, homelessness, brokenness...to a damp and dirty hillside cave, in a land and a time long ago...and yet, made startlingly present by his words and thoughts. As present as the faith which is his journey...and his journey's end. I love this book, and it is remarkable to me for this reason - it intrudes on my mind and heart, shakes me out of the numbness that can be everyday life, and reminds me - behold, a child is born... and to this reader, it is the very sound of redemption..."

--Rick Elias
Co-Founder, "A Ragamuffin Band"
Award winning singer and songwriter

<u>Dedication</u>

For Morgan,

The best gift I've ever received. The first little baby that
ever taught me about love. The reason I keep going,
when quitting would be easier. I pray that you come to
understand how much your daddy truly loves you…and
how much Jesus' Daddy loves you even more.

For Elise,
For friendship, encouragement, faith, and hope. You are
my best friend and inspiration. I pray this Christmas
season, you will find special moments with this
precious baby who comes to give us grace, peace, and
love without limits. You are the best mom I know, and
He would feel safe, and loved in your arms.
…and you would feel Him loving you back.

Thanks...

Pop and Jewell, Bob and Cathy, Rich and Dawn, Skip Denenberg, Tony Luke Jr. Brandon Kamin, Angelo Cataldi, The Kalas Family, Gloria and Stan Hochman, Dave Tiberi, Nick Bonsanto, Paul Ladd, John Willis, Pete Chivarou, The wonderful people of Crossroads Bible Church, Toni and Nick, (and Tuesday night Quizzo) Uncle Franny, Cousin George, Aunt Betty, Christine, and all the other Daliessio's I've met and haven't met yet. Brian and Lili Daliessio and Dominic. Linda and Rick Elias, for being my family in Nashville. Cindy and George Tuten and the folks at L.B.C. Cindy and Dave Lewis, Janet and Tim Britton and my home-away-from-home church, Crossroads. Cyndi Walker, Bingo, Hosie, Drew, Southside, HMH, JB. Liberty Hockey Alumni. For Ergun, Jill, Braxton and Drake, glad you are my friends. Peter Lumpkins, wonderful getting to know you brother. Tim Rogers and Tim Guthrie, Leo, Capps, Dr. Penn, Don R. Superstar. Battle tested friendship at its best. Michelle and Jim Freeman and the future little Freeman (my money is on JT^3) Angelo, Al, Rhea, Joe. Mark Sterling, my brother from another mother. Nicole and Barry and their soon-to-arrive little boy, congratulations, and I love you both. For Meredith Stafford who always thought I could do this sort of thing. It's a rare blessing that ones high school creative writing teacher can still be correcting ones homework! Allen Shamblin, my friend and one of the best writers I know, thank you for believing in me and saying so. You are what the word "gracious" looks like in flesh and bone.

For The Bergers, Steve, Sara, Heather, Siah, Cody and Destiny...for all you have meant to all of our lives. Terry and Mary Chapman...I miss you both, but I feel you all around. My grandmother, Dorothea Wray Shanko.

For Father John Sarro...God's messenger at the perfect moment in time.

And especially for Brennan Manning, for explaining grace better than anyone, anywhere, ever. You saved my life one November evening when your words poured over a broken and battered soul and showed me where the keys to the cuffs were.

And for Rich Mullins, the most ragamuffin of us all...a world you do not miss, misses you terribly. Thank you for the lesson about the stars having names...

Table of Contents

Preface

Why a baby? Why *this* baby?

I could answer this theologically I suppose. I could delve into the need for the savior to be born of flesh and blood so that His sacrifice would truly be equal to our sins.

Or I could go into the doctrines that involve his having to have a human nature in order to actually defeat a human nature. I could spend pages on exegesis that explains His having to enter this world as we all do. On propitiation. On what a sacrificial lamb actually is.

But instead I think I just want to make it simple…why a baby?

The first baby I ever held and loved with all my heart was born on May 7, 1998. She was 6 pounds 13 ounces and had brilliant blue eyes and thick black hair. The hair would soon turn bright blonde but the eyes remain the most beautiful blue I have ever seen.

She is my daughter. We named her Morgan Wray. Morgan because her mom and I really liked the name, and Wray because it was my grandmother's middle name.

My grandmother raised me until I was 5 and my mother got married. She was the first truly godly person I ever knew and her prayers kept me alive in the most turbulent times of my life.

Morgan was two weeks early but the doctors decided she was in perfect health and my wife had been struggling with preeclampsia and early contractions. The doctor decided it was best to induce and bring her into this world a bit early. She was born on a Thursday night at 10PM exactly. I was almost 34. I am a big man. I was a collegiate hockey player and have been an athlete my whole life. I stand 6' 4" and weigh around 250 pounds.

Yet that night as I held my precious little girl for those first halting few seconds of her life, I was reduced to tears and immense happiness mixed with fear filled my eyes. I was a dad now, a grown-up. How could I do this job? The giant was a little boy inside.

Babies touch us all in amazing and unique ways. Morgan's birth elicited a host of thoughts and a torrent of emotions in my soul that night. I was thinking and feeling a million things but only one phrase seemed to be coming out. For the first three hours of her life, after the nurses had cleaned her and examined her and she had briefly fed at her momma's breast, I held her and looked at her sleeping perfection and told her "I love you Morgan" probably every 30 seconds.

In my heart I think I was repeating it so that the first sound she became accustomed to was the sound of her daddy's voice telling her the only thing a parent *really* needs to say. I was rocking her slowly and softly and as I told her "I love you" a thousand times I was soothing my own raging heart. Because not once in my life had I ever heard my own dad tell me he loved me.

By this moment in my life I had not even met him yet. I grew up without him and it left a hole. A hole that this baby in my arms…this finest thing I ever did in my life…was now healing and filling.

It was safe to love her...this tiny little girl who looked just like her mom. It was safe. Something told me that in all my life of struggling and trying to get someone to finally love me for no reason other than who I was, I had finally found that love.

It was safe. She was tiny. She was innocent. She was perfect and she wrapped her little fingers around my thumb without opening her eyes, as if she had been waiting to do that for the last 8 ½ months. I could harm her so easily because she was helpless. One mistake would ruin a life. But all that just made me draw her closer to my chest, kiss her perfect forehead more frequently, and swear my allegiance to her protection until my dying breath. This baby had penetrated my heart like nothing else in all my life. *Just by being a baby.* And *that*...is why He came the same way my daughter did.

Jesus didn't arrive with fanfare and horn blast. There was no Secret Service and no public gala. He didn't just plop on the scene at age 25 with a nice job, cutting a dashing figure and riding a wave of popularity. He was a poor *illegitimate* baby.
Just like me.

There were whispers about the timing of his birth as it related to Joseph and Mary's betrothal. And the numbers didn't add up. Now here he was in a smelly cave where sheep had been bedding down probably just the night before. He was poor, unwelcomed, of questionable lineage, and wrapped in torn strips of linen...the way they prepared a body for entombment in his time.

But he was *God*. God as a baby! And he did what all babies do when we see them and touch them and let them work their magic on us. He melted the hardest of hearts. He brought tough, hard men to their knees, making smiling faces and cooing sounds. His cry touched the souls of anyone who happened to be there that night...just like any baby does.

There is something about a baby. Something about a new life and the way they react to us as if we have never done anything wrong or foolish in our lives. When I coaxed that first reactive smile from my daughters lips at around 6 weeks or so, I felt like a god myself. That little smile washed away 34 years of error and mistake and failed plans and broken dreams. It took away the sting of fatherlessness and of family shadows. It cleansed me and healed me and replaced my shame with pride and purpose.

That is why Jesus came as a baby. Because that is what babies do. It's universal. All but the most callous and criminal hearts will melt in the presence of a tiny babe. Babies are safe. Babies are innocent. Babies never pass judgment. Babies don't see our faults or our failures. Babies do best when we hold them and when we touch them...and that too is why Jesus came as a baby.

Because for 4000 years prior to His arrival man had seen God as a distant, harsh, tough, cold taskmaster. That wasn't God's fault. That was what the organizers of the time had done to Him. The preachers and priests and prophets who didn't speak for Him, (but who certainly claimed to) had pinned this burden on the people and created a God who could not be approached or loved or trusted to love us in the face of our humanity.

And He could not touch us because we were so afraid of a God like that. So He did the one thing that would surely break the image we were worshipping into fragments too small for us to rebuild.

...He came as a baby.

He came in the one form that nobody would fear. The one form that would not judge or ostracize. He came in the one way that would draw us to him irresistibly. He wanted to hold us and to be held. He wanted to touch us so he needed to let us touch Him. Only a baby could do that...

...only *this* baby

By this time, about 2000 years ago, Mary was 8 months pregnant. Here is a theological question for you...We know Jesus was fully God and fully man so does that mean he was fully God from conception? If so (I think so) does that mean Jesus was absent from Heaven for the entire 9 month gestation period? I never thought of that before, but it's interesting. If so...and let's go with this for the time being...did God miss Him during that time?

It's unlikely they communicated while Jesus was in Mary's womb. So did God the Father miss his Son? Did heaven seem a little less glorious during Jesus 33 year absence, especially during that period in the womb? Did God glance over at the empty throne at His right hand and wince, knowing what He had sent his son to do? Did He ever pace the halls of Heaven longing for the communion and fellowship He had always had with His beloved Son?

And what of Jesus? Was His spirit man limited by the human body He resided in? Was He more cognizant in the womb, than other babies are or was he like we all were? At what point did He become aware of what would befall Him?

There is so much to Christmas...so much we lose sight of when the tree goes up in the corner and the wrapping paper is pulled from storage. More than a crèche and Christmas carols. This is a wonderful story of an innocent baby, but it is the opening stage of the redemptive plan, after all. There was work to be done and that is why he came.

We know God looked down on Jesus and said "This is my beloved Son in whom I am very pleased" and that was from the spiritual, deity perspective. But I wonder if God ever looked at Jesus the man, and thought..."wow...He turned out to be a handsome young man. He reminds me of David..." We forget that God is a father...a dad. Dads are proud of their kids. Why not God?

I love this quote from one of Brennan Manning's books. The book is "Lion and Lamb; The Relentless Tenderness of Jesus" It was the second of Manning's books I read, after discovering him through "The Ragamuffin Gospel". I will only quote the following from Lion and Lamb...what follows will be my own thoughts. Brennan writes of the experience of discovering Jesus as He first appeared to us in His advent...

"The shipwrecked at the stable are the poor in spirit who feel lost in the cosmos, adrift on an open sea, clinging with a life-and-death desperation to the one solitary plank. Finally they are washed ashore and make their way to the stable, stripped of the old spirit of possessiveness in regard to anything...They have been saved, rescued, delivered from the waters of death, set free for a new shot at life. At the stable in a blinding moment of truth, they make the stunning discovery that Jesus is the plank of salvation they have been clinging to without knowing it!"

I think I read that selection a thousand times and never grasped the full effect until I was finally shipwrecked myself, and found that same plank at that same barn.

It is one thing to know, in my head, that Jesus was born a tiny, poor baby to a teenage Jewish girl who had not yet married her husband. The husband was not the boy's father and we pass those truths around as if they were nearly meaningless...as if God just put that stuff in the Nativity stories in Matthew and Luke so we'd have a nice warm feeling when we read them to our kids.

We also forget that we have the advantage of seeing Jesus in the light of history. The folks in the story were very real and they did not have that enlightenment. They only saw a pregnant teenage girl

19

and her husband whom she had not married in time to adequately explain the baby she was carrying.

Eyebrows were raised wherever they went in their hometown and so it is likely that the move to Bethlehem for Jesus' birth, while ordered by God, came as a relief to them both. At least in Bethlehem, nobody would raise eyebrows at the impending arrival of their first child. The hushed whispers of illegitimacy were not present in Bethlehem, as they were in Nazareth.

I found myself shipwrecked in the last three years. Shipwrecked in my career...shipwrecked with personal losses and identity losses...shipwrecked in my faith...and shipwrecked in my heart. In reality I was shipwrecked a long, long while before. When my wife left me and I was faced with part time fatherhood. As dreams died over the years and were replaced with the minutiae of necessary jobs, house payments and loneliness. I was adrift and alone and thinking that it was God Himself who had shipwrecked me.

I suppose that was my old teaching coming through. All those formative years of teaching me that I was not good enough or I had fallen too far. I thought He had attacked my ship and sank me out of spite, or disappointment. But what He was actually doing was preparing my heart until it was ready to be blown away by an infant baby in a stable.

I find myself washed ashore at the stable each December and I peer into that dank, cold cave and see the Savior... *The Savior*...lying in a feeding trough, surrounded by smelly sheep and smelly shepherds and wrapped in rags because his mom and dad were so poor that was all they had.

At this sight I am reduced to tears and silenced to wordless awe. One word creeps to my lips and it's all I can say... *Why*?" Why Jesus? Why did you love me so much that you would leave heaven and enter earth? Why would you willingly do it as a poor homeless infant lying in a trough? Why?" But that question is its own answer. Because He did this...because He entered this world this way, He draws me as no wealthy Savior ever could. Babies virtually demand our hearts. We can't help ourselves.

"Can I touch you, Jesus? Is this real or a dream? Can I hold you in my arms and look into your eyes and feel your infant fingers wrap around mine? How did you know this was exactly what I needed to melt my icy heart? You did this without words. You grabbed me with your silent, unspoken love and your absolute vulnerability. Letting me touch you in this way has opened the door and let you touch me...and I never saw you do it."

I drop my plank and stare at the beautiful face of my loving savior...who saw fit to begin his rescue and redemption plan for my heart, as a tiny baby, in a dirty manger, in a dark cave. I am shipwrecked...at the stable, enthralled by a baby.

...and this is the story of 24 shipwrecks, just like me.

Introduction

In mid November 2009, my daughter Morgan, who was 11 at the time, had a brief conversation with me. Approaching was the first Christmas ever that she didn't believe in Santa Claus. Sometime the past Spring she had discovered the truth. It was a passage that I regretted. I knew I would miss the days when my little girl looked forward to Christmas with childlike anticipation.

No more tossing and turning and straining to hear Santa's footsteps. I would never again climb to the roof as she was drifting off to sleep and stomp around and ring sleigh bells and do my best "Ho Ho Ho" and call out to eight reindeer plus Rudolf. I had done this since her first Christmas and it would be hard to let go of the tradition.

She wasn't a little girl anymore and she didn't participate in the mystery of the old fellow. It was hard for me to handle, to be honest. Christmas is special for me. I love making a big deal out of it. My family celebrates "la festa dei sette pesci" The feast of Seven Fishes, each Christmas Eve as is Italian custom. We have a special collection of Christmas Music that we play every year.

Bing Crosby recordings from the 40's. Sinatra, my friend Kim Hill's amazing Christmas album. And Christmas would not be Christmas to me without two great songs: "Santa Claus is coming to Town" by Bruce

Springsteen and "Christmas on the Block" by Allan Mann.

The other thing we never missed, until 2009, was having an advent calendar. I would buy two identical calendars, one for my house and one for her to keep at her moms'. We did that every year since she was two. This year she said she didn't care if we didn't do it. I was shattered. I had been through the humiliation of losing my home the 2 years prior.

My career in the mortgage industry was gone, my dreams were shattered. Christmas was coming and now it was going to be very different from all the Christmases that had gone before. For some reason the Advent calendar was a tough thing for me. It wasn't the same as Santa Claus.

I always knew she'd figure out the old guy eventually. I thought that one day she'd really appreciate the thoughts of me up on the roof every year with sleigh bells...except for that one year when I couldn't find the sleigh bells and I improvised by smashing a half gallon wine bottle in a paper grocery bag. It sounded remarkably like bells.

I assumed she'd one day have me doing it again on her roof some day as she lay down with my grandchildren and I would be extending my fatherhood just a little by providing wonder to them...and to her again in the form of a happy memory.

But the advent calendar was tough on me. There was no reason not to keep doing it. It's a cute calendar, I get it. But it actually represents something tangible in both Orthodox and Catholic Christianity, and it has jumped to many Protestant households as well. The truth is we all love Christmas and anything that can capture a bit of that childhood innocence is welcome in our world.

But Morgan didn't care to have an advent calendar and I was crushed. My little girl was losing interest in the traditions we shared and I was feeling old. It was sometime around Thanksgiving when this happened. It was cold and grey as usual and my heart was taking on a matching tone. Only one year removed from homelessness and still unable to find a decent job. Christmas was racing at me like a runaway freight train and I was staring at the approaching lantern in a stupor.

Life had been rough lately. I was really needing Christmas. Needing to be home and not in Tennessee. Needing to see my family, to see and hear and smell and touch the Christmases I remembered. I think more than anything…I wanted to really *share* Christmas with someone. I grew up without my dad and to this day we still have no relationship. I married and wound up divorced. I live for my daughter but only see her once a week and every other weekend. It seemed like love was a fleeting notion and a cold cruel mistress. And at Christmas it seems doubly difficult.

I was alone. Really, truly alone in this world. I think I clung to the traditions I'd created for that reason…because they took away that alone-ness. I was weary and I needed my soul to be touched by someone and something that would last.

That's when it hit me…I really needed an *advent*. I needed to hold Christmas in my heart this year and let happy memories heal the gaping and raw wounds that were causing me raging pain inside. I needed to reminisce.

The Advent is when we celebrate and reflect on Christ's coming to us. On his becoming one of us and taking on the form of a tiny baby. Able to be touched by human hands. The risk of being wounded was always present. He was born like all babies are born. He was tiny and frail and beautiful, like all babies are. He curled his tiny hand around Joseph's fingers like Morgan did mine in those first few hours of her life.

He cried and his little face turned red when he was hungry. He slept at the wrong times. His mother was weary and tired and she nursed him in the fog of sleeplessness. He might have had colic. His parents thought he was the most perfect thing they'd ever seen.

Every emotion we feel for our own children when they make their entrance into this world…Mary and Joseph felt for Jesus. We lose sight of this sometimes. We forget that He came as one of us. That he was *just like us*.

We go through that advent season without even considering what it means or what significance it still has in this world. Once each year, God builds into our calendar, 25 days to reflect on the deeper meanings of the nativity and the infant God-baby and we almost never do. We worry about Christmas lists and parties and plans and clothes and holiday decorations and which of our friends we aren't supposed to wish a "Merry Christmas" but rather an antiseptic "Happy Holidays".

...We have missed the visit.

By the time the calendar turns to the 25th we are so worn out that we have missed Him altogether. We either missed him or we never fully understood what it meant for God to put on the flesh of a tiny baby and come live amongst us. Why a baby? Why a poor baby? Can we really touch Him? *Can we touch him still? Will He touch us?*

That's where I was last year, approaching Christmas 2009 with a daughter who was growing up and a heart that was heavier than it had been at any holiday season in my life. I needed a visit from the tiny Savior. I needed to return to a day when this Holiday meant what it used to for me. I needed to be happy.

I needed to somehow enter into that nativity scene and behold the tiny baby with awe. I needed to have a fresh encounter with the divining moment in all of history. Like Brennan Manning, my opinion is that Christmas is the holiest of the Christian Holidays. More special than even Good Friday or Easter. Because the only thing more amazing than Him dying for me...is Him coming here for me in the first place. But come he did.

I needed Him desperately. Especially that year when my life was a disaster. I needed the *cry of a tiny babe.*

I started really thinking about the advent in a different light. I started seeing the players in the original nativity in a new way. Mary, Joseph, the baby Jesus, those shepherds. All the main characters in a vast play that initiated the great plan of redemption. I sat there in 2009 with a full understanding of how it all played out. I had--as all of us have-- seen it from this side of the Cross. I understood it because I can look backward and see it all unfolding.

But what did they know then, those members of God's cast of characters present on that Holy Night? How much did Mary grasp at her tender age? She was just a teenaged girl. She had a brief visitation from an angel and the next thing you know she is giving birth to a miracle baby.

Joseph was probably a man in his mid twenties. He just wanted a wife. He hadn't figured on all this scandal and outrage and whispered accusation. It took an angelic visitation of his own for him to trust Mary's crazy story and not divorce her. There must be something special about this child she is carrying, he thought. But what? And is it worth my reputation? What if I don't *like* this child after a few years?

Joseph was just a guy...like I am. I am sure he asked questions of himself that I would have asked. All these years later and I missed his humanity. Why did I forget he was human? Or that Mary was still a kid herself? Or that the nativity scene was probably more likely to have taken place in a cave than a somewhat welcoming stable as our revisionist version goes.

I began to wonder how much the players really *did* understand. I stood here 2000 years after this birth seeing both ends of the redemption plan. I understood what Jesus life would bring. I knew why He came. I fully comprehended who he really was. I knew words like Calvary, and crucifixion, and cat of nine tails were as much a part of this beautiful story as angels, and stars in the east, and Magi. I knew this silent night would one day yield to a dark Friday afternoon, a hopeless Saturday…and a Sunday that would snap history cleanly in two like a saltine cracker.

But the longer I thought about it, the more I was convinced that none of the players in the little alabaster crèche I set out under our tree each year understood any of that. They were a mom and a dad, and some smelly shepherds who had seen a star, heard a celebration in the sky and came to see what the fuss was about.

They were an inn keeper who had no idea who he was turning aside. And maybe some passersby who saw the ruckus and poked their head in the filthy cave to see what was going on. They didn't have any idea what the future held for this little boy, except maybe a life in a carpenters shop, and whispers of illegitimacy.

But I did have an idea. I closed my eyes that November morning and imagined being there amongst all the commotion and comings and goings. I saw myself an observer in the shadows, watching the scene unfold with full knowledge of what the next 33 ½ years would hold. I imagined what it would be like to visit this scene on the very first nativity…*and hold my Savior in my arms.* To look at his tiny hands and feet and understand…where his own mother did not…that these hands and feet would be torn open by rough spikes.

I could hold him to my chest as I did my own daughter, and feel the *very breath of God on my face.* All it would have taken was for me to have been there that night. To have been an active witness to the first

29

advent. To have been in a place to have touched the face of God himself. I just had to be close enough. That's all it would have taken.

I started wondering what effect that would have had on me. On others I could also imagine meeting this tiny God-child. Before long I was there...in the shadows of a cramped sheep cave. Watching history being defined and being touched by the tiny newborn hands of God in the flesh.

...this is where our story begins. One year ago...in the waning days of November 2009, I wrote the following journal entry...

"In a few short days December 1 will be upon us and the season we call "Advent". It comes from the Latin "adventus" which means "coming".

I love this time of year. As odd as it sounds, I love the cold gray days of November and December. Skies that threaten snow, but withhold. A sun that barely filters through the dim for days at a time. I wouldn't want this year-round, but I like the seasonal occurrence. My friend Rick has the same opinions. Having grown up in southern California, he likes this dreariness for the simple change it brings. For me, growing up in the Northeast, this weather signals the coming of winter and the advent. When I was a little boy, for a little while at least, we had advent calendars each year.

Starting December 1st, and through Christmas Eve, I, or my brother Tom, would peel open one of the little doors and see what picture was behind. Usually it was a fireplace or a Christmas tree or some wrapped packages. On December 24th, it was always a smiling Baby Jesus in a manger with Mary and Joseph nearby.

I loved the advent calendars and it was one of the first traditions I began with Morgan when she was old enough to know what we were doing. That and me stomping around on the rooftop with those sleigh bells pretending I was Santa.

I want that advent...that coming. With the massive upheaval that has befallen me for the last three years now, I am longing for more of Him. Not from a structured theology standpoint...although I am pursuing bachelors in religion right now. Not from a "whatever the trends are in Christendom these days" standpoint either. I don't really want the Jesus of pop culture preachers...thank you just the same. I want an advent. I want a head-on collision with the infant King of Kings. I want what it must have felt like when those smelly shepherds were startled by a star and then by angels and found themselves falling on their faces in front of a newborn little boy in a stinky barn, sleeping in a feed trough. That was my savior and that's how He chose to come...that was his advent.

Poor, destitute, unwanted by even the innkeeper, and with considerable questions about his lineage. Born to a poor carpenter and his teenage wife. On the run from birth. From the City of The King (Bethlehem) to, literally, the city of trash, (Nazareth). This was the advent of Jesus. This is how he came to us.

Having lived homeless, as I did for so many months, and now having just finished up my New Testament Survey class and understanding more about Jesus' life from a historical aspect...I was asking new questions at Christmas. Why would He leave all that for this? Why be so poor and homeless? Why this advent...this way?

I know that events in the last few days have left me desperately wanting to know Him as I never have. If I will love anyone or anything else on this earth... I must first and foremost love Him. I must desire him above the love of my daughter or a future spouse, should God see fit. I have to love Him more than all my plans and my dreams and my desires. If I will ever love anyone who needs love...I have to do it the way He did it.

I have struggled for so long with this. I have literally reached my hands up to heaven in the hopes that I could feel Him reaching back down, always to find myself frustrated as I couldn't feel or even imagine what the loving embrace of Jesus must feel like. For some reason, today...early in the hours of this gray Sunday...before Church or even breakfast, even before the sun tried its feeble battle against the gray curtain of sky...He showed up and grabbed me tightly. Why today...why now? Why this advent? I don't know.

*I am hoping He is preparing me for a future. Teaching me to receive love. Whatever it is...I thirst for him like life itself right now. This King of Kings who forsook all that title offered, to become a 'man of no reputation" and be born in a barn, grow up in "the city of trash" and die on the landfill of Jerusalem with spit running down his face.*That was His advent too.

I am looking forward to December 1-24. I am looking forward to His advent in my heart again and again."

And so our story begins...

Chapter One

"It just doesn't seem like Christmas"

Wick Radcliffe was chattering in broken Chinese when I turned the corner off Arch Street. He was standing in the doorway of his tiny book shop, talking to his neighbor. It was amusing to me to watch him attempt the Mandarin dialect as he did. He was animated and loud and his neighbor seemed mildly amused at his efforts. I was nonetheless impressed...God knows I couldn't speak the language of this neighborhood.

Arch Street is the main thorofare of Chinatown in Philadelphia. Wick's store is on a small side street that runs perpendicular to Arch. It's really almost an alleyway. My sister had discovered Wick's shop on a walk from her house to her job at a coffee shop about 3 blocks away.

She liked the uniqueness of his store and the fact that he specialized in Christian titles. He was one of maybe 2 or 3 shopkeepers in Chinatown who was not actually Chinese or Asian. Wick had found his little shop quite by accident and the rent was very low and he liked the area. Over the years he had gotten very friendly with his neighbors and considered them family.

Stoic Wilson Radcliffe was from the Main Line area of Philadelphia. He came from money and his family had been prominent Presbyterians in a predominantly Catholic town. His parents had given him his very unique name because his mother wanted something that engendered a strong demeanor, and his father was a self-styled philosopher and so the Stoics were a favorite read. His middle name of Wilson was shared by his father's favorite author and preacher A.W. Tozer.

Wick hated his name. "Who names their kid 'Stoic'?" he asked me once. As early as he can remember he wanted something else but he never could convince his parents to let him change it. Shortening it to "Wick" was as close as he could get. As for living up to their "*good chrustian expectations*" as he would say in a forced drawl, (making reference to the classic line from Flannery O'Connor's "Good Country Folks"), Wick never followed his families piety. He discovered Jesus after waking up in a gutter in the middle of February in Dewey Beach Delaware, with no recollection of how he got there.

Somehow Wick had gotten a copy of Brennan Manning's "*The Ragamuffin Gospel*" and had his face to face meeting with the Christ of God. Manning is his favorite author. During our first meeting, when he discovered my fondness for Brennan, he pulled out a worn paperback copy of the first printing and opened the page to reveal "*To Wick...best wishes, Brennan*" written in purple crayon.

Before I could ask, he explained that he crossed paths with Manning in the Philadelphia airport and neither of them had a pen. The only thing they could find was a kid with a single purple crayon and a five page coloring book that was provided by the stewardess from United. Wick loved that story.

Today was November 30th and a typically cold grey day in Philadelphia. I was home for Thanksgiving and had journeyed up the highway to my hometown and the familiar sights and sounds. I stopped in at Tony Luke Jr's for a cheese steak and a hug from the owner. I visited with Tony for a half hour and then headed to Wick's shop, not really knowing what I was looking for. I knew I wanted an advent calendar for my daughter, because each Christmas we did them and I wanted to keep the tradition going.

The truth was I wanted to visit with Wick because Wick is a true ragamuffin. A broken life who never forgot what Jesus Christ really did for him when they met, and who had never really wandered far from what made him such a rascal in the first place.

It had been a very hard two years and I always felt better about my own humanity after spending an hour with Wick. I don't know anyone who is more appreciative of who he was, who he is, and what could have been if not for God's intervention in his life. Wick grows on you.

I wasn't ready for the coming Holiday's and that worried me. I am a "Christmas Guy" as my friends say. I get into the Holiday season like few others. From mid November to January 2, I am one big happy Italian, who can't get enough of traditions and sights and sounds and smells. My family celebrates "Feast of Seven Fishes" on Christmas Eve and I have a very specific list of Movies, TV shows and music that must be played during the season.

Somehow this season had snuck up on me and I wasn't ready. In the past two years I had lost my house, my career and my possessions, when the mortgage industry collapsed. I was a mortgage banker and had been for ten years. But by 2008 I was homeless and living in a 1995 Volvo hidden behind a church.

I stayed in Nashville TN (where I now live) because my daughter is there with my ex wife and I have to remain in her life. Otherwise I would have come home to Philly and never looked back. I like Nashville just fine. But Philadelphia is home. This year I was sad as Christmas approached instead of my usual joyful self. Walking down the little side street to see my friend Wick, I knew one thing: *I didn't know what it would take to make me happy again.*

Wick greeted me as I turned the corner and he smiled and pointed at me and said something funny in Mandarin to his Chinese neighbor. They both laughed and the Asian man looked at me with mild awe in his eyes. "What did you tell him Wick?" I asked. Wick smiled and was about to answer when the Chinese man spoke in halting English, "Mr. Wick says you are far to rarge a man to have such a dispreasant rook!" I smiled and the Chinese neighbor laughed. "How you get so big?" he said with a straight face. I stared at him for a split second and then felt an involuntary smile crossing my lips. "You're playing with me right now...aren't you?" The man broke into peals of laughter and I felt myself relax a bit. Wick spoke up as he reached his hand toward mine. "This is Mr. Xiao. He is a professor of English at Temple" I smiled and reached for Wick's hand, "its Engrish" Xiao said with a chuckle. Something about that made me laugh deeply and he extended his hand to me. "You can call me John" he said in a voice and pronunciation as perfect as radio announcers. "John...nice to meet you." I offered.

Wick, John Xiao, and I stood in the street for a few moments as the day grew dark in a hurry. It was around 4PM and sunset was upon us. Inside the caverns created by the skyscrapers, the shadows grew even faster. A lull in the conversation allowed me to ask Wick the question on my mind. "Wick...I am looking for an advent calendar. Something a little more substantial than the cheap paper things I can buy everywhere around here. Do you have any?" "Yeah I might have something..." Wick said with a smile.

John walked in with us and we grabbed cups of coffee and walked to Wick's crowded and overflowing worktable. Besides retail sales, Wick was recognized as a master in restoring old texts. He had re-covered an old Bible of mine three summers before and he was always wanting to show me his latest rare first edition that he had discovered in a yard sale someplace for a nickel and was bringing back to life.

Wick didn't have a book to show me this time, he was busy working his way through "*Davita's Harp*" by Chaim Potok and hadn't had a restoration project in about two weeks. He pulled out a box of Advent calendars and showed me each one. There were a few of the traditional paper calendars with the little door that you open each new day for the month of December. There was a fabric calendar with 25 pockets sewn in, one for each day where you inserted a little reliquary or symbol of Christmas.

There was a wooden version that dated back to about 1928 and was hand made in Lancaster County Pennsylvania. None of them sparked my interest and none of them seemed to have what it took for me to get back whatever it was that was missing from my Holiday season.

Wick was puzzled and didn't think he had anything that I would really want. "What are you really after?" he asked me. "I don't know Wick…something that would take me back to when I was a boy. Something that will get my daughter back into the spirit. This is the first year she doesn't believe in Santa and it is sort of hard for me."

Wick laughed at this. He had never had any children of his own but had befriended my daughter when she was about age 4 and she referred to him as "Uncle Wick". He knew Morgan's love for the season and her love for her daddy. His laughter hid a sadness I could detect in his eyes. Wick is my friend and he understood that I was hurting this year after all I had gone through.

"Have a seat Craig" he said, and he, John and myself walked over to three huge leather chairs and sat down. "Okay...tell me what's really the matter" Wick said. Before I realized it, I felt hot tears welling in my eyes and I looked at my shoes instead of looking my friend face to face. "Wick", I began. "I have never felt so lost...not in my whole life."

Wick, sat back in his leather chair almost to the point of lying down. He had known most of what I had been going through over the last 3 years and he was concerned. But somehow he suspected that my current state wasn't just about the losses I had been enduring.

"Craig we've been friends for a while, and I know you well enough to know that this isn't just about losing your home, or your job. This isn't about being homeless. This is a lot more." I was silent for a while and suddenly the words poured out like water bursting a dam. "Wick" I began, "I just feel so lost. I feel so sad and so sorrowful. It's almost Christmas, usually I am happy beyond belief right about now but I just feel sadder. I am not living in my car any longer but I have never felt more homeless...more alone in this world."

Tears were flowing now and I was silent for a long time with my eyes closed. I was thinking about my daughter being "too old" for Santa. It had all happened so fast...those first 11 years of her life. Being divorced from her mom since Morgan was 2 only accelerated the

41

passing of that time. How many bedtime prayers had I missed? Too many for my liking.

I was thinking about my fatherhood and how I treasured it and then I began thinking about my father. I have only met my dad once in my life…when I was 43. He desires no relationship and I have stopped trying to have one. I have the rest of the family and I am thankful for that.

But still, the Holidays are a time for family and being together and here I was about to be alone yet again. I said all this to Wick and to John Xiao and they just absorbed it like sponges without saying much at all. Wick was thoughtful as he finally began to speak, "Craig…it's no mistake you are here looking for an advent calendar. You really need an advent." He could tell by the look on my face that I wasn't following him.

"Adventus" he said. "Huh" I offered quizzically. "Adventus…it's the Latin word where we get 'Advent', it means Christ's "being amongst us". I wasn't following the line of thinking and Wick said, "Jesus entered this world as one of us…exactly as one of us, the same way we do…as a baby. Have you ever wondered why he did that?" "I've thought about it some," I told Wick. He knew I was a Brennan Manning fan and he knew I had read "Lion and Lamb" by Manning. "He came as a baby so we would find him accessible and approachable. So we wouldn't be intimidated." Wick nodded approvingly. "He came vulnerable so we would understand that His place in our lives is totally at our mercy, He would only enter where we asked him" I said...more to myself than to Wick.

I hadn't noticed that Wick had walked to the other side of the room and when I "snapped out of it" he was standing next to my chair with a box in his hand. John Xiao was smiling approvingly and he nodded toward the box in Wick's hand. "Take it" John said. Wick handed me the box and before I opened it he began to explain, "Craig this is a special advent calendar...but I can't tell you why." That was a strange statement for Wick to make and my puzzled look betrayed me.

"John has had these in his family for 78 years. Supposedly everyone who has ever displayed this calendar over the holidays has had a special encounter with Jesus during that time. The encounter varies and seldom does anyone talk about it. Apparently it can be so deeply moving that others would find it hard to believe anyway. John and I think maybe you need this." I could sense the enormity of this gift as Wick handed it to me with John's approval.

The calendar wasn't a lot different than all the other advent calendars I had seen. It was much nicer than the paper versions available in stores and supermarkets. It was leather, like a book, but it had no pages. The cover had 25 small hand made doors that were hinged with tiny leather strips.

Whoever made this went to great effort. It had the words "ADVENTUS" in large block letters burned in the leather at the top. Each day was marked in script. It wasn't a typical dark leather, but was about the color of a baseball glove...a light tan. It was more a work of art, to me, than it was a calendar or a Christmas reliquary. It must have taken a very long time to make and it was obviously a labor of love. It seemed mystical...in the truest sense. As if somehow God had visited this little handmade calendar. If Christmas really had a spirit...this calendar contained some of it.

"It's perfect Wick" I said. Wick was smiling broadly, almost knowingly. "Yes...yes it is" he answered. "How much?" I asked and when I did he smiled again. "There is no charge, because you can't keep it. When the Christmas Advent is done, and Epiphany has begun, you have to return it. It is the only one we can get and next year someone else will be needing it." He said that as if he knew all along that this was the exact calendar for me. As if the entire afternoons conversation was just a test to see if I was ready. Perhaps that was exactly the case.

John and Wick and I talked for a few more minutes. Maybe a half hour in all. Then I took my package and headed out into the chill Philadelphia night looking for my car and feeling the faintest glimmer of hope that this Christmas season would be special after all. This beautiful calendar seemed to spark something in my heart. I couldn't wait to show my daughter.

I drove out of the city and across the Benjamin Franklin Bridge on I-95 south. I was lost in thought, as I frequently am when I drive. I saw the exit for highway 291...the old "Industrial Highway". That used to be the only link into Philadelphia when I was a child. I95 ended in Essington back then and you had to get off at the Boeing plant and take 291 past the Westinghouse factory and into town. I thought about exiting and driving down 4th avenue and past my grandparent's old house but it was already dark and there wouldn't be any point to it.

I miss the house sometimes. My grandparents are long gone but I spent so much time there that that it was like home to me. Especially at Christmas…when I always turn to thoughts of home and family and when living in Nashville feels like living on the moon. The memories associated with the house on 4th Avenue weren't all good, but there were enough good ones to make it call to me as Christmas approaches.

When I am home I stay with family and on this trip I stayed with one of the two families who had 'adopted" me years before. Bob and Cathy DuHadaway had first met me when I coached their son Bryon in high school ice hockey. They quickly became friends and then my family. I lived in an apartment over their garage for about 3 years and I still stay there sometimes. On this particular trip home in 2009, that's where I was.

I turned up the drive and pulled my car to the back. I grabbed my package and walked first to the house before going to the apartment. I wanted to show Cathy and Bob the wonderfully unique advent calendar I had gotten on my trip to Philadelphia. They were sitting in the kitchen when I walked in the back door.

"Look what I found today Cath" I said I pulled the handmade calendar out of the bag and showed her. She marveled, as I had, at the detail and the loving way this calendar was put together. We talked for 15 minutes or so and then I excused myself for the night.

I walked across the driveway to the doorway leading up to the apartment and felt the cold sting of freezing rain drops.

The November night sky was spitting hesitantly and I paused to look up. Somewhere above that grey canopy was an early winter moon. I could see the light as it spread across the top side of the cloud cover but was unable to find a break and penetrate the night.

Something in this occasion made me sad. Like there was some light somewhere that needed to touch my soul and illuminate my own darkness and it wasn't able to get through to me. The clouds became symbols of something holding me back. Not sinister necessarily but restraining. I waited in the night...very still...hoping for something to change and the moonlight to find it's way through, but all I felt was the infrequent droplets hitting my face.

I walked to the door and up the stairs to the place I had called home for 3 years. I set my bags down at the top of the stairs and called my daughter to say goodnight. I sat in the big easy chair and waited for her to pick up. "Hi daddy" she said...as she always does. "Hi honey!" I replied. 10 minutes of exchanging stories about her day and the upcoming holidays and finally I got to the real purpose for my call...the calendar.

"Guess what I got us today?" "What?" she asked me. "I went to Uncle Wick's shop and found a really amazing hand-made Advent calendar. So this year we can do it again and it will be very special...it's really amazing. Mom C saw it and she loves it. Morgan calls Cathy "Mom C" and considers her a grandmother.

Morgan didn't say anything and I was instantly wondering why. "Don't you think that's just amazing?" I asked. "I guess so" she said. I waited for a minute...a long time when you have nothing to say..."You don't really care to do the Advent Calendar this year...do you?" I asked her. Her long pause answered without words. "I don't care...it's okay I guess"...she said.

I knew right then I'd lost this one. She'd outgrown the Advent calendars too. We talked for a few more minutes but I scarcely remember what we discussed. I told her I loved her and I would be home in two days. We hung up and I sat there in the darkness with just a small table lamp across the room. This was not going to be the holiday I had hoped for and I was beginning to really dread the upcoming Christmas Season.

That was unlike me. I was always a Christmas person. I never wanted to lose that trait and here it was, after losing so much personally in the past few years, now I was losing a beloved tradition too. It was too much for me. I sat there for a long time.

Hours passed. The clock struck Midnight at the old Ukrainian Orthodox church next door and I realized it was December 1. I fumbled through the bag and picked up the beautiful calendar that only hours before had held such promise. Now it was yet another symbol of disappointment and the changes my life was enduring.

"Well...it's December 1...I suppose I should do this anyway" I said to nobody but the darkness of the room. I opened the little leather door on day 1 and found...

December 1

No Reputation...

I opened the little leather door and was stunned by a torrent of memories of years past. All the times I had opened an Advent calendar door as a child, and again as a dad with my little girl. The memories were as fresh as the smell of a Christmas tree.

My Christmas season memories start out with getting ready for school. It's early in the morning and we are getting dressed for the walk in the cold...struggling to put our boots on over our shoes. Our mom has wrapped our school shoes with wax paper to help them slide into the boots easier. This works, but the problem is the wax paper gets torn up when you take the boots off at school and you still have to get them on in the afternoon.

My solution was usually to either not wear the boots or take off the shoes and wear only the boots. I think to myself how that's a funny memory of this time of year.

I Open the first little door on our advent calendar and see...

Jesus...the infant Savior

Advent really begins and ends with Jesus and so does this advent calendar.

Its review I suppose but there He is...a tiny baby in about as "Un Savior-like" a situation as can be. If you were searching for a Savior for the world, the last person you'd think you'd find would be an illegitimate baby lying in a feeding trough in a cave with a teenage mom.

The last thing you'd think you'd see would be fanfare provided by some local shepherds who look and smell like...local shepherds. If you figured the King of Kings was arriving with full entourage and secret service...you would have missed Him altogether. Yet here He is. Unassuming, totally approachable, intimidating no one and wooing every heart with His innocence and vulnerability.

The unmistakable power of the baby in the manger was that He blew open the door of access to God. He did it by entering this world the same way we all do...and by allowing Himself to be as vulnerable and touchable as all babies are. And by doing what all babies do...making us smile, touching our hearts, giving us hope.

The great songwriter Steve Earle wrote these words about 15 years ago in a song called "Nothing but a Child"

Once upon a time in a far off land
Wise men saw a sign and set out across the sand
Songs of praise to sing, they traveled day and night
Precious gifts to bring, guided by the light
They chased a brand new star, ever towards the west
Across the mountains far, but when it came to rest
They scarce believed their eyes, they'd come so many miles
And the miracle they prized was nothing but a child

Nothing but a child could wash these tears away
Or guide a weary world into the light of day
And nothing but a child could help erase these miles
So once again we all can be children for awhile

Now all around the world, in every little town
Everyday is heard a precious little sound
And every mother kind and every father proud
Looks down in awe to find another chance allowed

Babies do exactly that for us. They bring us second chances and third chances and more chances than we could ever dream in our wildest imaginations. They are brand new starts every day of their lives.

There is something miraculous about holding a baby…particularly if you have never done it before. The way they look at you…*they way they see into your soul*. Babies, especially those only minutes or hours old, have no preconceived notion about us as we hold them. They don't have the slightest idea about our past, our failures, and our secrets. They only know what they see before them right now…just like Jesus has been telling us for 2000 years. That He has removed our sins from us as far as the East is from the West.

That is why…amongst other things…God chose to give us glimpses in two of the four gospels, of Jesus as an infant baby. Because he wanted to make certain that we got it. That we understood why he allowed His son to enter this world the way every one of us has.

He wanted us to all find ourselves here at this dank, cold, musty cave where His own Son would meet us if we would come find Him. Where He would lay in our arms, silent, vulnerable, precious and loving…and longing to be loved, handled, held, and touched by us. The creation coddling the Creator. The ultimate act of trust, vulnerability and loving invitation.

Jesus was as much a human infant as my own daughter was…or as your child. He needed to be burped after he ate. He made messy diapers that made his parents laugh at their volume. He slept when Mary wanted to be awake and he was wide awake when her teenaged body was worn out and needed to rest. He blew spit bubbles without knowing he was doing it but laughed anyway. He smiled instinctively at the sound of his mother's voice. He probably had dark hair that had a mind of its own.

All those wonderfully precious moments that mean so much to parents of newborns…Jesus provided them to Mary and Joseph. Maybe so much so that his parents occasionally forgot the angels and the voices from God and those visions and dreams. He curled his tiny hand around Joseph's finger more than once and reduced his stepfather to tears of joy, fear, and feelings of unworthiness.

When we come to this manger…in this cave…and we see this infant for ourselves, it changes everything. All those images of God as a lightning bolt throwing, angry, mean spirited God have no place here. This baby destroys the unforgiveness that we have attached to this wildly forgiving God.

Men may have spent 4500 years teaching us that God is mad at us, hates us, punishes us and loves it; but in one moment that forever splits history, the infant baby Jesus demolishes that image and replaces it with that of a tender little boy, hours old, reaching out to wounded hearts bound in fear of judgment. Jesus came here and took on the form of a baby. Not just any baby, but a poor, illegitimate, scandalous child who would grow into the "Man of No Reputation" that Philippians 2 tells us about. He became *nothing*.

You can't fear a baby. Period. A baby wasn't around when I did those things I am so ashamed of…he is only a few hours old. His memory begins and ends with me holding Him. He touches me in my deepest wounds and darkest places and his touch sets me free.

That's what babies do...especially this baby. God knew that. He knew that to break down the walls of fear and shame that man had built between him and us it would take something amazing and special and miraculous. So He collected his thoughts and said "They've had 4500 years of seeing me as mean-spirited, angry, harsh, and distant. They need to see me as I really am...crazy in love with them. I know what I'll do...I'll go and live amongst them. *And I'll come as a baby*...so they'll see me as I really am...touchable and wanting to love them". Who can resist that?"

I think it worked...
Welcome, Savior

December 2

Saint Nick

I suppose it's ironic...or poetic that the character I see when I open the door on December 2 is Santa Claus. Ironic because in the Christian circle I formerly tread, Santa was anathema to us. He was here to rob us of the true meaning of Christmas. He was a tool of the devil. It's poetic for the same reason...

When I was growing up, I attended a pretty closed minded legalistic church. They went looking for "sin" anyplace they could and they squeezed it out of some pretty bizarre places. Playing rock records backwards, (don't we all?) telling stories about women who wear pants getting leg-cancer, you know...good solid theology.

Anyway, one particular target was Santa. He was secretly trying to displace Jesus...He was the spawn of Satan... (If you rearrange his name you can actually spell Satan!*gasp*) He was the leading cause of over commercialization of Christmas...good solid factual objections.

I loved the old guy. I still do. I loved reading Clement C. Moore's "The Night before Christmas" when I was a kid. I watched "Santa Claus is Coming to Town" in clay-mation and never in all that time did I once think of him as displacing Jesus. I never thought of him as dimming my view of that little manger or the star in the heavens or the real reason we celebrated. In fact, it was made clear to me that he did what he did every Christmas Eve because he loved Jesus and did all this in His name.

Otherwise he could have picked any night of the year to fly around the world and slide down several billion chimneys delivering toys. In fact...if he wasn't trying to do it all on Jesus' birthday, he could have sent the packages by Fed Ex and turned the reindeer out to stand stud at a breeding farm.

No, Santa was all about Jesus and I knew it. We all did. Nowadays with Christmas under attack the way it is, Santa might really be our best ally. I mean we are still allowed to talk about him freely so why not go ahead and use him as a springboard to talk about Jesus? When some kid asks, "Why does he do it all on one night?" we can go into Santa's reasons for that *particular* night.

You see...I see Santa as a Jesus worshiper. I see the whole story as a way of explaining that Ultimate Gift. In my mind he doesn't take away from Jesus...he adds to His fame. This legendary man does what he does because that's how he keeps Christmas in his heart. If anybody tried to hijack it and twist it away from Jesus, it was us. The Santa legend wasn't designed to refute Jesus it was about making Jesus famous. Maybe we ought to take it back. Maybe we should, as I suggested earlier, use Santa as a witnessing tool. God used a talking donkey once, skeptics.

I was proved right as I watched him walking up to a little cave in Bethlehem, removing his red wool hat, pocketing his pipe, checking his red suit for appearance. He is a large man, so he has to bow his head so he can get through the doorway, and taking his place on his knees next to the manger where the poor, homeless, infant-savior lies only hours old. He leans in on the little sleeping figure and his eyes well up in amazement.

He is silent for a long time and when he speaks he whispers a hoarse whisper..." You should see the happiness I brought in your honor tonight, my Lord. I did the best I could...but I am not you...I hope you are pleased." Then Santa's shoulders quake a little as the tears flow a more freely..."I didn't bring you anything. I went through my sack and there was nothing I had that felt appropriate, nothing worthy. So I only have my love, and the contents of my heart. It is you who brings me the joy I give others. It is you who is the Source of my wonderful laugh. I am the giver of gifts on earth but I do not compare to the gift you bring, sweet child. My only gift to you is my worship and my love...and to let you love me as you desire."

The old man remains quietly on his knees a long, long time, enraptured and lost in the miracle of the infant Savior in the feed trough. Even in the hustle and bustle of the commercialized, unChristianized world...Santa finds a place amongst the shipwrecked at the stable.

I find myself chuckling silently as I watch this. Christians especially get so worked up about the "desacralization" of Christmas. I detest the whole "Happy Holidays" thing too but have we *really* removed Christ from this day? Does that mean that for all these years we were actually dependent on WalMart greeters saying "Merry Christmas" when we walked in the doors, or is that just a handy excuse for the fact that I have lost touch with the advent?

Do I care that my daughter doesn't have a "Christmas Party" at school anymore? Because she has yet to forget it is Christmas. These thoughts race through my head as I watch this legendary figure lost in worship and holding the key figure of all of history in his red-suited arms.

Each Christmas season, the greatest Christmas special ever made plays in prime time. "*A Charlie Brown Christmas*' has run each year since 1964. Each year the beautiful bubbly flow of Vince Guaraldi's "Linus and Lucy" will resound once again as the "Peanuts" gang dances around Schroeder's piano.

Charlie Brown will be unable to reign in his charges, he'll pick that pathetic little tree and at the height of his despair, he will let out a call *"Isn't there anyone...who knows the real meaning of Christmas?"*

And then the moment that reduces me to tears every year like clockwork. Linus will take center stage and say "Lights please" and then he will recite the nativity from Luke chapter 2 verbatim. On national TV. In prime time.

I can't wait to find out some day how many people wound up finding their way to the stable and to a face to face relationship with Jesus because of that little 2 minute interlude. This nation may not be the bastion of Christianity it once was, but we still know why we really celebrate Christmas. Linus never lets us forget.

That was why I never got worked up about Santa Claus with my daughter. Because Jesus Christ is powerful enough to withstand being deposed by a fat man in a red suit. It isn't even close. Ask a child the true meaning of Christmas and the vast majority will tell you about Jesus. Maybe their theology is off but they know who the central figure in history is.

Everyone does. Santa, elves, reindeer. It makes no difference. The answer to the question of "Why does Santa do all this" has not changed. He does it to honor the ultimate gift.

Now some traditions I miss and should never be messed with. Kenny G should not supplant Frank Sinatra singing Christmas carols. George C. Scott was never the Ebenezer Scrooge that Alistair Sim was.

Bruce Springsteen sings the greatest version of Santa Clause is coming to town. Ever.

But the one truth about Christmas is Jesus. While they don't always admit it, everyone knows it. And at Christmas, even Santa bows at the manger and is changed by the touch of a tiny baby.

And tonight, for whatever reason God saw fit to allow me to bear witness; I have seen the heart of this giant and legendary figure as the real reason for his existence has come to light. He is touched by this baby, as he was when he Nicholas of Myra and saint of the early church whose acts of kindness inspired this legend.

...to honor this baby

December 3

Joseph

The figure behind the leather door on my advent calendar is no mystery. He is the step-father of the son of God. Joseph is kneeling beside the manger where his tiny boy lay sleeping.

He stares for a long while at the little baby sleeping in the straw. He turns his head and glances at his tiny teenage bride exhausted and sleeping on a pile of dirty hay. He feels his rugged face turn crimson.

This has been a hard year for Joseph. This girl was his promised bride and a year ago they were betrothed. This year the marriage would be completed and consummated. But somehow Mary wound up pregnant. She told Joseph about it first, before she told anyone else.

Joseph considered ending the betrothal right then and there, but he has a kind heart...and deep in his heart he loved her. Still, this sort of thing will ruin her reputation and that of the baby. And it would doom him as well. He has a struggling carpentry shop and he doesn't need to be the butt of innuendo and private jokes about his wife and son.

Still...the way Mary told him the story, about the vision, and God speaking to her. He was almost convinced to believe her anyway and then God spoke to him in a dream of his own. He confirmed what Mary had said and so Joseph took her into his home and decided to let people think what they wanted.

Now here they were in Bethlehem because Caesar wanted to tax all the Jews and he wanted them to go to their hometown. It was Mary's hometown too...both of them were in David's lineage after all. They started off with other members of their family but because Mary was so far along now, they couldn't keep up with the caravan.

By the time they made Bethlehem, all the available rooms were gone. They knocked on every door and even asked some relatives who lived in Bethlehem for a place to sleep. Maybe it was because of Mary's condition...or maybe it was the rumors that were flying around about the baby...whatever the reason, nobody had a place for them. All they could find was this cave. An empty hole in the side of a hill where a couple of dozen sheep had been staying. They had to crawl into it and they could barely stand up. It was dark and dank and cold and it smelled terribly.

They didn't have time to clean it before Mary went into labor. Joseph had never seen childbirth before and he was scared. They didn't know a midwife and so he and Mary just had to figure it out as they went. Mary's tiny body was wracked with pain and at one point Joseph thought he'd lost her. Eventually it was done and their son was born. In all the commotion neither of them heard the angels outside.

They only found out about them because a few hours later, some local shepherds stopped by to worship their son and they spoke of a star in the night, and a host of angels telling them about Jesus. There were four of them. Their stories were incredible.

Joseph was considering all of this as he knelt by his tiny son's cradle. He reached his hand in and touched the sleeping boy. Joseph whispered as to not wake his tiny wife.

> *"Jesus...I am humbled. I hardly know what to say to you. I believe now...I wrestled with it before but now...I believe. Truly you are from God and this was all part of some plan of His. I don't understand. The shepherds speak in terms of "Messiah" and*

"Savior" and "Emmanuel". That means "God with us", my son. Is this true? Are you really God in the flesh? Are you the Promised One?" Joseph pauses and collects his thoughts, *"I am honored to take this role in your life. I always wanted a son. I will do my best to be the best dad I can be. I will seek the will of your Father as I raise you, and try my best to be a blessing to you. I feel so unworthy. I am sorry that this is all we had for your birthplace...we are very poor...I have nothing to offer you."*

Joseph chokes back a few tears at this point. He is still a man after all. He is a husband and he loves his wife and he has grown to love this boy. Like any man, he wanted better for his family but timing and poverty were against him.

The baby stirs and cries softly. Joseph reaches down and picks him up and pulls him to the folds of his robe. He kisses the baby Jesus on his tiny lips and he feels the softness. He whispers" I love you my son...my Lord". The baby seems to smile the slightest smile and then falls asleep in Josephs arms with his head pressed against Joseph's heart. Joseph closes his eyes in a prayer and rocks his boy slowly...he is thinking. Thinking about the twists and turns his life has taken in the last year or so. Thinking about the tiny woman sleeping in the straw. Thinking about this child and all those dreams and visions and this place...this cave.

Being a stepfather is difficult enough, but to be stepfather to a child who the angels have proclaimed the Son of God? To have no defense against the whispers...at least no defense anyone would ever believe. This is a lot for any man to bear and this man is just like any of us. But somehow holding this child tonight gives him the courage and the determination to do his very best. Like anyone who loves children, this man finds a love growing in him for this baby and his resolve to be a great dad for him is firm. He will do the job God has called him to do, and history will reveal his success. He is Joseph... Jesus' earthly dad...and the whole circumstance has left him shipwrecked at the stable.

December 4

Grandparents Day

It's colder this morning than it was yesterday. Christmas is definitely in the air. We are putting up the tree this weekend.

I examine my advent calendar and glance at what I have seen so far...Jesus on day one and Santa on day two, interesting intentional irony. Yesterday was an emotional meeting with Jesus' earthly father Joseph. That one spoke to me deeply.

Opening the little door for day 4, I see one lone figure kneeling beside the manger and holding the infant Jesus. She is rocking him slowly as he sleeps and she is singing him a lovely song in a beautiful voice that sounds very familiar. It is lilting and sweet and it seems to call to me from over the years. I think I know this woman, but it is hard to tell.

She leans close to Jesus and gently strokes his forehead, the way grandmothers do.
She makes no effort to hide or even control her tears. She is safe with this infant-king and she knows it. She has been with him in heaven now for almost 17 years but she makes this pilgrimage in her heart each Christmas. Somehow, this time, God saw fit to let me witness it.

She is beautiful, like the pictures that I recall from my childhood. That's why I think I know her. She sings a song I recall from those years ago. I know this song.
She possesses a most beautiful singing voice and this morning she is singing a lullaby to her Savior and it is the most amazing and beautiful sound I have ever heard. It brings her peace to offer this to Him...this baby-King. It brings her redemption, too. I realize that I know this woman...and I watch through many tears.

As long as I knew her...for the first 30 years of my life...she loved this Child. But one mistake in her past haunted her and she wrestled with His love for her until, quite literally, her final breath. I was there and I remember. In the days before she went home to Him...she sought reassurance, even after walking in her Faith for over 40 years by that point. He gave her what she sought and her words as she departed were amazing...she was reaching out her hand toward a Savior only she could see and repeating "Oh Lord my God...Oh Lord my God" over and over. And then she was with Him.

Now here she is again...young, pain free, beautiful, and without shame or guilt or doubt about her eternal safety. She leans in on the infant and I hear her singing to him. It's a song she used to sing to me when I was a little boy growing up in her house. It's the song she wanted to sing to the children she left behind in one moment she regretted for 60 years. She could never find forgiveness from those children, but this child offers it freely and she is giving Him the best gift she has to offer...her love, in the form of a song.

I can't remember the name but it sounds like "Jesus loves me ...or Jesus Loves the Little Children...and there are strains of "Haven of Rest" in there too. It's an old hymn that she used to sing all the time...and that I sang back to her at her funeral. I would give anything to enter this scene and hug my grandmother one more time but I can't. Even if I could I don't think I would. This is her moment with the infant-Savior and I can't disturb it. I am privileged to observe it and I will leave it at that.

Her hands caress the boy in the trough and I see they are no longer bent and gnarled by arthritis, but straight and gentle and soft. Her shoulders aren't stooped from the shame she carried about that one decision she made 70 years ago that she never could forgive herself for. She has peace now. Peace with her Savior and her memories.

This is the grandmother I knew and the one I didn't know. This is Dorothea Wray Shanko, my daughter's namesake and the earliest example of a Christian I would ever see. Perfect and completed in Jesus.

There is a man next to her, and I recognize him instantly and he has the same thick shock of black hair he always did. That was a family trait that I carry too, except mine is brown. I've always looked like him, but the way he appears this morning...the resemblance is uncanny. This is the man I saw in his Navy pictures when he was a Seabee in WWII. He is the handsome man I saw on the deck of the *"Donna-Kay"*, the gorgeous 32' Cabin Cruiser he once owned. He is tall and strong and clear eyed. He isn't haunted by his tortured life or his pained memories of his immigrant childhood.

He isn't chained to a bottle anymore. He is free from the demons that stalked him and stole his life. He is my grandfather, Albert Shanko...everyone called him Jake. He is kneeling by the manger, like he did once in the kitchen of the house on 4th Avenue when I was asleep in my coach and he didn't want to wake me up and he got on all fours and crawled out unseen. An amazingly soft and gentle gesture for so gruff a man.

He isn't ravaged by alcohol now. He is whole and perfected. He is strong and his shoulders are straight and his smile is wide and unmistakable. He reaches into the manger and touches the little baby softly. In that touch he finds the forgiveness he needed all his life. He offers the gentleness to this baby Savior that he never had for his own children while he walked this earth. He gives this infant king the love his heart always held but never felt safe to show.

He never had the chance to ask forgiveness when he was alive but he has found it anyway since then. Here in this cave...shipwrecked at the stable...he is the man he always hoped he could be, but never was. He is the grandfather I would have loved to have. He came to this baby only a few scant weeks before he died from cancer, so in many ways he is still getting acquainted with him. The manger brings him healing and hope.

The two figures look at each other and it is different than any look I ever saw while they were here on earth. It is a love I have never witnessed. Not a marital affection anymore, but a completion. They are both loving this baby and that is their bond now. No more co-dependence, no more needy, impassioned strife. They are both who they were always meant to be and so much more.

This is the only way they could have found redemption as a couple and individually. They are unified by a baby in a manger. I see them in a way I never saw when they were on here on earth. It would have been a wonderful model to witness. I am happy to see it now.

This is what a baby does...He changes the beaten and downtrodden and wounded into worshipers. He sobers the intoxicated with the intoxicating power of his love. He surprises you at the reactions He draws out of your soul. But only when you find yourself shipwrecked in his presence and you know you are a ragamuffin.

December 5

Meeting the Baby Myself

Before I get the day going, I decide to open the little door on the advent calendar and see what is behind it. Every day has brought another unexpected scene this season. Things that were not behind the little paper doors of the little advent calendars I had growing up. But scenes that are inseparable from Christmas anyway

...even if they seem disparate. Peeling back the leather I see...myself.

I have been to this cave as an observer, today it is my turn to kneel at this dirty manger and see my infant king.

I can't get over the roughness of this cave. When I was a boy, the nativity scenes always seemed fairly hospitable and almost welcoming. "I know it's a barn and everything...but this isn't so bad" I would think to myself. Jesus wore a smile and there was a crowd of well dressed and important looking people around him. Mary looked healthy and much older than she probably was in reality, and she looked as if, rather than just giving birth to a baby in a barn, she was ready to run to the all night grocery and bring back hor' dourves.

The truth is, this place depresses me. It's cramped and the ceiling is low. I am 6' 4" and I have to practically crawl in here. Mary and Joseph aren't nearly my size so they can walk hunched over, but even then it is uncomfortable. They won't be leaving for days, because neither she nor Jesus should be moving around right away. So they will have to endure this mess for a while.

It is deep and roomy enough for a few adults but it is so low. I am claustrophobic to begin with so maybe that's just my personal take on the matter.

Mary and Joseph are sleeping and I crawl over to the manger in the alcove. He is there, looking up at me with loving eyes. I want to pick him up and yet I am afraid. But having observed the previous visitors here, I know He wants me to hold Him. He wants this because that is how babies transmit their love to us, when we hold them.

When we touch them, we let them touch us and Jesus wants to touch my soul tonight. So I pick him up. He is wrapped in strips of linen and while its hard to keep that all in place, He seems to be quite comfortable. I bring him to my chest...right next to my heart. I search for words. I feel a hand on my shoulder and I look to the right...it is Joseph.

"Talk to Him" he says. "No" I whisper, There is so much I want to say but I am afraid" "Afraid of what, son?" Joseph answers, "*He is a baby*". I know Joseph is right about this but yet I am paralyzed in awe. I held my own child the night she was born and for the first three hours all I could manage was "I love you" repeated over and again. This is Jesus...the Son of God. What words can I say? "What language should I borrow to thank thee...dearest friend" was how the hymnist once put it.

Jesus is above my meager words, and yet my heart aches to talk to Him. The need to open my soul to this baby Savior is greater than my fear and shame and so finally I draw a deep breath...

> *"Jesus"* I whisper, *"I hardly have words for this moment. I feel so unworthy to be here with you. And yet somehow we have so much in common. Holding you like this...right now. I know what fate awaits you. I know the cruel violence you will have to endure to redeem me. I don't like thinking*

*about that with you in my arms. I
understand a few things better tonight,
now that I've touched You. I grew up
under the same shadow of illegitimacy
as you will. I have been homeless as
you one day will choose to be. I have
been separated from my father too. I
have so many hurts inside that I need
you to touch. It has been a tough few
years and I am weary. I miss the
innocence of youth and I miss the
promise of a life yet to be lived. I wish
I could return to my childhood, and
have a second chance at some things".*

The baby smiles at me and coos softly. I think He understands. I think too, that is why he came as a baby. This infant-Savior doesn't care what my past may have held. He doesn't care about my failures or my shortcomings. Those things mean nothing to Him at all. He is only a few hours old and so that's all the history He knows.

That is the wonder of His coming to us as a touchable, loving infant baby. His love is penetrating when we take him to our hearts and let it do what it does. I hold Him for a long, long time. My sadness and regrets turn to hope and worship and joy. Babies can do that. Babies bring the new start we all desperately seek from time to time in our lives. I am lost in the wonder of holding a child and I am enchanted.

"Jesus" I continue, *"love is such a confusing thing sometimes. Help me to love you first and most. Help me to become the man you have in mind for me to become. Help me to bear your name well on this earth. Help me to seek out and find those tragic souls who wander this world desperately trying to find this cave and this manger...and You. You have touched me little one...please use me to touch others in the same way. I remember...I remember that cold night in November of 1990 when I was so lost and so hopeless and so ready to..."*

My thoughts grind to a halt as I recall the night I first encountered this child...the desperation of my life, the loss of hope...the fear...the way the gun barrel felt, just for a split second, against the roof of my mouth. I recall the way I heard him calling to me when I thought he would have rejected me and hated me instead. I recall the loving touch I felt when I was weeping and pouring out my heart to Him that night.

I am holding Him now as a baby and I am thinking about all that would one day befall this tiny child. The beatings, the torture, the cross...for me. My heart rips open and I want to scream "No!" and to somehow stop the inevitable outcome of Jesus' life. But I know I cannot. He came to do that, and all my life I had overlooked the fact that the brutalized figure nailed to the cross was once a beautiful little dark eyed baby boy that I could hold. I am undone in love and worship and sorrow all at once.

I close my eyes and offer silent prayers. Prayers for people I love and want the best for. Prayers for people who I will one day meet who don't know this baby. Prayers for dear loved ones who carry heavy burdens because they are more afraid of God than I was and they have not been here to see this baby in a long time. Prayers of thanks to God for coming to me in this form...touchable and seeking to give me His love.

I am moved and transfixed. With eyes closed, I am memorizing the way this little baby feels as I hold Him, so that whenever this life gets me bogged down with failure or concern, I can recall this moment in detail...and feel this new beginning again. Holding this baby, I am not a failure, not illegitimate, not a man who struggles with receiving love and giving it away. I am not unforgivable or stained beyond cleaning, or useless.

Here with this baby in my arms, I am a child myself. And the Father of this little baby is very fond of me indeed. Only a child could calm the turbulence in my heart. Only a baby could soften the blows that life had so frequently struck against my dreams. Only a baby could convince me that there is a Love in this world that is greater than even the worst of my failures. Only this baby in this manger...in my arms. I am shipwrecked at this stable and lost in the wonder of what that really means.

December 6

Folks I Know

Seeing my grandparents here just a few short days ago was moving. It touched a core of longing and sentiment in my heart I had long ago buried. Perhaps it is missing them as I do, coupled with the built-in feeling of home and family that Christmas evokes. But this time of year it is not unusual at all to find myself caught up in memories of family and friends who have moved to their eternal destination.

Today it seems like most of those folks I love and miss have come to visit this baby king. When I open the leather door on December 5, I see a host of those folks. The first is a couple, much like my grandparents, who are kneeling in worship and I instantly know who this is.

It's my friend Terry who only recently moved on to heaven. His beloved Mary is with him and he is wide eyed at the little baby. This is his first pilgrimage to the manger from his home in heaven. He walks in with determined steps...the bent shuffle that Parkinson's had left him is gone. Seeing the redemption story now...now that it is completed in his life...is overwhelming for him and he is instantly on his knees in worship.

Terry served this baby as a pastor for all of his adult life. And he lived as one of the greatest examples of what this baby can do in a life that anyone has ever known. It is good to see him able to worship this baby again in a healthy body. His back is strong and his speech is clear. Mary kneels with him and together they adore this little child. Their first Christmas together in many years. Mary went to heaven several years ahead of Terry and he longed for her during their separation. She is smiling and vocal, not silenced by the Parkinson's that had affected them both.

They take a long and enjoyable time with this baby, giving him the love they held in their hearts for so long...and the love they will rain on Him for eternity. There is no hurry to leave and there is feeling of time passing. They spent their lives in service to this child, and they had seen all that His touch could do in their lives and in the lives of thousands of people whom they ministered to. Now it was just Terry and Mary again, worshipping the Christ-child as they did when they first began their life together.

They were like parents to me, and I wish I could stop time and spend it in this moment, watching my two dear friends in their completed faith, but time will not permit. After a while, Terry and Mary leave the cave and I see some other folks entering.

The next visitors move me beyond tears. My soul is torn and for the first time I wonder if I will reveal myself simply by my own emotion. The first of three visitors enters the cave. My tears flow hot down my cheeks. It is my little sister Collette who went to heaven 13 years ago in a car accident shrouded in mystery to this day. I can barely stand seeing her without my heart breaking. I have missed her more than words can express.

She moves very determinedly to the manger and reaches in to hold the tiny baby in her arms. Collette always loved children and they loved her back. She was a natural pied piper to little children and had dreamed of being a pediatrician. Those dreams were altered when her car was run off the road one notorious April night. It's a night I will never forget and I miss her every day.

I watch Collette with the baby for several long reminiscent minutes and I am remembering her smile. Her wit and her crazy sense of humor. I was her unofficial big brother. Her parents had taken me in as a member of their family when I was a lost soul with no one to care. Collette loved having a big brother and I loved having a family at last. Her moving on to heaven was hard on me and even harder on her family.

I am thinking these very thoughts when a couple approaches the cave from the opposite side as Collette entered. They come in with the combination of hope and sadness in their eyes. They both have the most expressive eyes I have ever seen. I realized that on that fateful April night when I walked into the kitchen after an 8 hours flight home and saw them trying their best to hold their hearts together in light of the worst news a parent can ever hear. This is Bob and Cathy...Collette's mom and dad.

They come here in celebration of the baby each year, as we all do. But each year something extra comes to greet them. The child is the bringer of hope and the one who would one day swallow up death until it held no power at all. This is a hope that this couple comforts themselves with even after 14 years of grief. Because of what this child did...and does...in our hearts, they have hope that they are never really far from their precious Collette.

Merely three days prior to the accident on that dark highway, she had come to the stable and discovered herself a shipwreck. She had accepted this child and given Him the best place in her heart. She was introduced to the child in the office of an evangelical Catholic priest named Father John. That was on a Tuesday. Just 40 minutes into the following Saturday morning Collette was in the presence of this child King. If anything could offer comfort to a grieving mom and dad, it was the knowledge that their child was ready when the time came.

But here, on Christmas Eve, there is no room for, nor trace of sadness. There is hope and healing and even a few smiles. Cathy kneels by the manger and she sees the baby Jesus in the arms of her daughter and she knows the scene is just as it should be. Collette would most certainly be one to take special care of this tiny king. Bob smiles and wipes the tears from his eyes and looks with pride at what his daughter has become since she entered the presence of this king of kings.

I am speechless but my mind is racing. It is ironic to me that this baby that both the child and the parents are worshipping, this baby is actually the reason there can be a reunion at all. Jesus came to defeat death. The hopelessness that death leaves us with when faced without Jesus, that is what he defeated. He "swallowed up" the power of the grave. Collette is not "dead", at least not in the ultimate sense. She is very much alive because this baby was willing to die in her place. That is irony and love intertwined.

Collette leans in against her mother as she holds Jesus closely to her chest. It would almost be what you'd expect if Jesus had been Collette's own child. There is a certain peace and serenity that is evident in this picture. For one day each year, this child can connect us to those who have moved to another place. He himself crossed that gulf and crossed the bridge. God has wondrously allowed them to reconnect each year at Christmas through the offering of his own child. "I love you" Collette whispers to her mother and father as she returns Jesus to his cradle. Cathy and Bob have tears of their own as they whisper those words back to their beloved little girl. I mouth the words from the shadowy corner where I remain unseen..."I love you Collette...I miss you".

The three figures...three of the people I love more than any in the world...move toward the door. Collette leaves and turns to the right and to a light as bright and powerful as anything I have ever witnessed. Bob and Cathy watch her walk off before turning left and returning to their home and their family. Collette's sisters and brother and their families. The brilliant light fades and seems to render the cave even darker. I watch as if watching a sunset.

All night tonight there will be other visitors. People from my past. People who have gone on before and who return and who are still very much alive in my heart and in this world because of the life and eventual death of this tiny baby. They live on in another realm, in the presence of God. But this baby has taught me that the distance between them and us is not far at all, it is merely a heartbeat away.

They come from all over heaven, to see the work of redemption. For us it begins here with this baby, but for them they are seeing it's amazing, loving completion and their perspective is unique in ways I don't have words to describe.

They were shipwrecked once, at this same stable and it was here they met this child-king. Now they return to see Him again. Only their worship and praise is different because they are complete. The work is done in their lives. But still they come to the stable...no longer shipwrecked, but just as moved and just as in awe, and just as full of worship as they were on that first trip here. Here in this dark cave, and this straw-filled feed trough...and this little pauper-prince.

December 7

No Place Like Home

I open today's little leather door on the advent calendar and I see...a cave. A cave?

Having grown up with the usual, stable-oriented Nativity Scene, I never once thought to question its accuracy. It's a 3D version of bumper sticker theology, I suppose, accepting that tradition as fact. But I never had reason to doubt it and to be honest; it doesn't change much about the scandal of this event in history. But for today...it will be explored.

Jesus was not born in a stable as we have been taught. It wasn't somehow warm and welcoming and full of nice clean straw and a smattering of animals gazing lovingly at the infant Son of God. They didn't just come off the set of "Charlotte's Web" and the big sheep wasn't speaking with the voice of Dave Madden. Farm animals are basically spooky and reticent. They don't come and eat out of your hand like a puppy. And they aren't remotely clean.

But the real fact here is that Jesus wasn't born in a stable at all. It was a cave. If you go to Bethlehem they have a cathedral built on the site, but the archaeologists will tell you that it wasn't anything as ornate or beautiful. It was a cave. A hole in a hill with one very low doorway.

In those times, shepherds would round up all their sheep at night and run them into a cave. Then they would lie down in the low entryway so no predators could enter without first awakening them. It is the image Jesus presents when he talks about "My sheep hear my voice ..." He describes Himself as the Good Shepherd who lies down in the gate and if the thieves try to break in and lure away the sheep, they must do so by coming in some other way.

Such was the case here. The cave was probably big enough for maybe 30 sheep so it was somewhat roomy for only two people. But it was low, because sheep are small. Mary and Joseph probably could not stand up inside the cave. The doorway was only big enough for a couple of sheep to enter at a time...or one adult who was willing to bow down and probably crawl in on all fours.

It was dark and damp...as caves are. And it certainly hadn't been properly prepared for childbirth. It probably smelled like sheep. Sheep smell terribly. For one thing, they are a notoriously dirty animal. Their long coats collect everything from everywhere they have been. They need to be sheared twice a year not only for the value of the wool, but because the filth that clings to sheep wool...particularly around certain areas of the sheep...is disgusting. They have bugs. They have lice and ticks. They are sloppy eaters and the little trough that Mary used for a crib was probably a disgusting mess.

Before my daughter was born, her mom went on a cleaning frenzy in our apartment. The place smelled like Clorox and Lysol for about 4 straight months. It's common with pregnant moms-to-be...they call it 'nesting". Imagine poor Mary...she is just a teenager of probably no more than 16. She is technically unmarried because the Jewish custom took a year from betrothal to actual consummation and she had gotten pregnant during that period. They were poor. It took a dream from God Himself to convince her husband that this whole Messiah story was true.

Now she was about to give birth, a scared kid in a strange town under scandalous circumstances, and she finds out only hours before delivery that the place is a disgusting mess. What could she do? We forget sometimes that all the players in this grand plan of redemption were real humans and they felt all the things we feel. Sometimes, because we read about them in Scripture for all of our lives, we remove their humanity. But they were real people.

I remember how scared I was when I found out we were going to be parents. I wanted to be a dad. I looked forward to children, yet when the little test strip turned blue, I was petrified. So was my wife. Why would I think Mary and Joseph were any less?

Most moms' have a special bond with their unborn child. Sometimes I have been guilty of removing that emotion from Mary. I see her sometimes as a player in this play and not as a young girl who carried a baby for 9 months and felt all the same attachments that all other moms feel.

By this moment in time Mary was in love with her little baby and she was fully engulfed in the nesting thing and I imagine that when she crawled into that cave on her hands and knees and saw a dark, dank, smelly hole in the wall with dirty, soiled straw everywhere and a trough with some stagnant sheep-drooled water laying in it...she must have broken down in tears. "Oh Joseph...we can't have Him here!" she might have said. A poor, meager carpenter, Joseph must have tried to force a smile and convince his young bride that everything would be alright. He probably tried to fix it like a man would and his best efforts only put an exclamation point on how bad this place really was.

Maybe Joseph finally took Mary into his arms and kissed her head and said "I know it's bad...but it's all there is Mary. We have a promise from God and our child will be okay." Maybe as he held her, he hid his own embarrassed tears. I know how he felt.

The really amazing thing here is that this was the place God chose for His son to enter the world stage. This stinking, nasty hole in the side of a hill. This cold, dreary, dark, smelly cave. Probably as far removed from a hospital maternity room as ever could be.

This is where God's great Plan of Redemption would begin. Why? Why was Jesus born this poor? Why was He so rejected by men that He even had to be born in a cave like this? Why? And why a baby in the first place? Because one glimpse at these humble beginnings and no one can feel threatened by this Savior. He wasn't rich, He wasn't powerful (in the worlds eyes) He wasn't intimidating or daunting. He didn't demand the accolades due Him. (Phil 2:5-8) He was a "Man of No Reputation". He "became nothing" (again, Phil 2:5-8) he wasn't a name-it claim-it carnie huckster selling some promise of riches and wealth as we determine it.

He was lowly, broken, and humble, He was frightened. He intimidated nobody. He wanted what all babies want in those first few hours and days...He wanted to receive love and more than that...He wanted to penetrate our hearts with love as only holding a newborn can do. That is why He came as He did.

To gain access you have to be willing to bow down. Maybe even get on your hands and knees if you are tall like me. There is only one way into this cave and this King. There is only one entrance and it requires you to leave everything behind and bow. You won't be impressed by the surroundings. He did that on purpose.

When you get here you will feel like a welcome guest because few people will make this journey and come to this humble place. But those that do...those that allow themselves to be shipwrecked at this place will walk away changed to their very core.

By a baby in a feed trough in a cave in Bethlehem.

December 8

No Room

These are the some of the hardest days of the year for a kid. Christmas is coming...you don't feel like going to school and when you get there, everything is pointing towards Christmas. Your friends talk about their wish lists and you count the days until Christmas break. Who can learn in that?

So this morning I open the little door on the advent calendar and it's a man. An older man who's face I do not recognize. I don't know who he is or why he is standing outside the cave where Jesus is lying in that manger. He seems to really want to go inside but he is hesitant. He has been here before and was unable to get past this point. There is something about coming face to face with the baby-Savior that freezes him in fear.

Finally Joseph comes out and offers his hand. The old man looks bewildered at Josephs offering of friendship and he pauses a long moment before reaching out. The man's eyes stay sullen and focused on their hands...he won't look Joseph in the eye. Joseph reaches in and whispers something in the man's ear. I can't hear the words but I see a look of relief, mixed with sadness on the man's face. Joseph motions toward the low entrance to the cave and the man bows down in order to enter, almost having to crawl. I walk over to the doorway and peer in, unnoticed but curious.

The man sees Mary in the corner, sleeping on some straw with her coat laid over top. He breaks down into tears. "I'm sorry Mary...I'm so sorry. I had no idea...I didn't know." Mary rubs the sleep from her weary eyes and smiles a wistful smile. "It's okay...really. It's okay. We are okay here and we appreciate your generosity..." "No" the old man says with a wave of his hand, "It wasn't generous...it was convenient and nothing more. I had my own quarters at the Inn and my children are grown and gone and so I have extra rooms, and I could have invited you there but I didn't. I didn't realize..."

Mary has walked slowly to the man by this point and she takes his old gnarled hand in hers, "Sir...you gave us this place, and we needed a place right away. It turned out okay...we are fine. He is fine..." With this the old man breaks down in sobs. He'd been worried. He was sleepless after seeing the star and those shepherds showing up. He knew he'd made a mistake and he only now understood the gravity of his error. "If I could do it again," the old man whispers between tears, "I would give you my own home. I would have invited you in".

Then it hits me...I know who this man is! It's him...it's the innkeeper! The first man to say no to Jesus! *"What is he doing here?"* I wonder to myself. (As if I have any more right to be here than he does) The old man is struggling to keep his composure. The weight of his decision earlier in the evening has hit him full force. He struggles to find words in the face of Mary's tenderness and Joseph's welcoming forgiveness.

Finally he clears his throat and says, "You said He is fine...could I see Him?" Mary smiles lovingly and touches the old man's hand. "Of course" she smiles, He is right over here..." Mary leads the innkeeper toward a small cut-out in the cave, where the manger has been placed. The innkeeper lowers his head as Mary pulls back a small coat, hung over the doorway to give the sleeping infant some darkness and privacy.

The man is slow to raise his glance from the floor. Mary senses his trepidation but maybe she senses some kindness too. She touches his elbow and whispers "It's okay...really". Her voice is soft and gentle and almost lyrical. It breaks the last vestige of hardness and shame and embarrassment that the old man held and he begins to cry openly and freely.

He drops to his knees by the side of the manger and looks at the sleeping Savior of the world. His sobs are muffled but audible none the less. Maybe he had a dream or maybe seeing the star and the humble visitors coming and going throughout the evening made him realize who this was who was actually sleeping in his sheep pen.

Whatever it is, he realizes it now. This child is special. This child is from above, and he had the chance to offer him his best and he turned him away. Maybe he knew instinctively he would forever be known as the innkeeper who said "No Room".

Whatever is ripping through his tortured brain...he is sorrowful over it. He wipes the tears from his eyes and looks up at Mary and Joseph. "I have four children...all grown now. I have 17 grandchildren so...I know how to do it, and I was wondering..." "Of course", Mary interrupts, "Of course you can".

The old man smiles broadly through his tears, and reaches into the manger and lifts the infant King into his tired arms. The baby stirs and opens his dark eyes. The man breaks into soft tears as he draws the little bundle into his chest.

The old man's beard is long and a few stray strands touch the baby's arms and he looks quizzically at the unknown object. The man whispers softly as the baby nestles into his robe..."I am sorry...I am so sorry. I didn't know...I just didn't know who you were or why you came. I had such a chance to give you *something* and I didn't do it. I wish I could have that moment over again. I would give you my best, little baby...my best".

The man's tears fall unapologetically onto the manger where the infant king was lying just moments before. A long minute passes and then the baby reaches up one tiny arm and touches the man randomly on his lips. The baby holds a stare for a long while and the man softly kisses the tiny hand that has explored the place where the whisper was coming from. In that moment the man is undone.

The mistake of not giving Jesus a place weighs enormous on him now. He says it one more time in a voice hoarse with sadness, "I am sorry Jesus...sorry I didn't make a place for you". The baby yawns the tiniest yawn and falls back to sleep.

The man smiles a slight smile as the love of this child penetrates his chest and into his soul, and suddenly the old man turns to look me in the eye with a desperate and piercing gaze..."Tell *everyone* about me...no one should ever say no" he says. Placing Jesus gently back in his manger, the old man stands up and walks off into the night.

December 9

The Shepherds

I have had to take a long time to digest what I have witnessed thus far. I know this child has the power to heal, to bring hope, and to restore happiness. But I've seen him do so much more already. These mystical visits have been emotional to say the least.

I have been looking a long time at the calendar in my hands. The bells of Sts. Peter and Paul Church have tolled again and a new day dawns. I've been sitting here a good while, pondering the meaning of what I've seen.

I gently open the next little door and a smile makes its way across my face. This scene is one of my personal favorites, and I've been waiting for this one!

...The shepherds have arrived!

They were tending their sheep out in the wilderness outside of Bethlehem. In fact they had their flocks penned up in caves much like this one here. They were asleep in the doorway of their pens, as shepherds do, and they were startled awake by a brilliant light and the sound of a chorus of angels. They heard one voice above the din and it told them that their Savior had been born tonight in Bethlehem. They saw that wonderful star in the heavens and they followed it to this place.

A bewildered look is evident as they approach the cave entrance. After following the fanfare and angelic direction, they were surprised to see that they have arrived at a sheep pen just like they left behind. This is not exactly the way they thought a king should enter the world.

There are four of them...which some might find odd. I always thought there were three. Then I remember that the Bible says there were three wise men from the east, but all it says about the shepherds is that there were "at that same time, shepherds, living in the fields, watching out for their flocks at night..." I think over time the numbers got juxtaposed and tradition became three shepherds.

There are four of them here and I noticed that three of them have brought gifts. The other man brought nothing and he also is the quiet one of the bunch. They bow and enter the cave and bring their gifts to Mary and Joseph. I was standing nearby and decide to listen in on the conversation. The first man brought bread, the next brought eggs and cheese, and the third brought wine. The fourth man had no gift and seemed disinterested in the small group that had gathered around Joseph and Mary.

The conversation was polite. "I like how you've fixed this place, Mary', the one shepherd says, "I never considered actually living in a sheep pen." Another shepherd remarks about how Mary has managed to get the place clean enough for a baby delivery in such a short time. The other man remarks about her health, is she okay and do they need anything? The conversation is pleasant...like what you'd hear at a housewarming or a cookout. "Do you need a job Joseph? Because I know a guy who knows a guy..." "How long will you remain in Bethlehem?"

Time ticks by and not much is actually said. The shepherds fall silent after running out of pleasantries and suddenly one of them...the fat guy who brought the bread...notices one of them is missing. "Where is L'enchante?" He asks. I don't know," replies the eggs and cheese guy. "L'enchante!" they call out.

But there is no answer. Then in the silence they hear a whispered song coming from a dark corner, away from the oil lamps light. They bring a lamp with them and they see worn boots sticking out from under the makeshift curtain that separated Jesus' little alcove from the rest of the cave. They pull back the curtain and the missing shepherd is there. It is L'enchante..."the enchanted one".

He is holding the baby Jesus to his chest as tears fall from closed eyes. He has a smile on his face that defies description...he is "enchanted" indeed. He rocks back and forth slowly on his knees, in the soft cold mud of the cave floor.

He is singing a song softly, as a whisper, under his breath. It is a song of love for his infant-Savior. "Jesu...Jesu...Jesu...Jesus...Jesus" he is lost in worship and adoration and caught away in love with this wondrous baby-king.

He has forgotten about all of us and this cave and the presents he never thought about bringing. He has only this moment with this child and he is making the most of a chance to love the Son of God...and to let the baby love him back. The baby is smiling as I have never seen a baby smile.

There is a connection between them...a flowing back and forth between the Giver of love and a man who really understands how to receive it. He does nothing. He lets Jesus pour his love into his heart and does nothing but reflect it back in worship. This makes Jesus very happy and His tiny face shows it.

We all remain silent as we watch L'enchante loving his Savior, and being loved by Him. L'enchante got it. He came with nothing. He didn't get sidetracked by small talk and nonsense. He felt no sadness or embarrassment for his present state as a smelly shepherd. He didn't make confession first for any sins he carries inside. He went straight to the baby in the manger and fell on his knees and let the baby do what babies do...love us.

I am dumbfounded. I want that heart for myself. I want to be swept away by the baby in the manger who so deeply desires that I hold Him and love Him and let Him love me. In that moment I understand why Jesus came as an infant.

I am 47 years old. I have seen love disappoint and let me down, as we all have. People who were supposed to love forever, without condition have failed to do so. Each time we try to find it, we run the risk of getting hurt and wounded once again. Love that flows from people to people will always be flawed because we are flawed. It is hard to love each other...plain and simple.

We wonder if the other person is sincere, or if they will endure once they know our faults, or what if they go away once I drop my guard and let them love me?

But a baby never poses those risks. Infants are totally free with their love. Babies don't know about our past and they don't care. They don't see us as ugly or sinful, or liberal or conservative. They don't mind our bad hair days or our frumpy clothes. They don't mind the smell of dirty sheep on our robes.

They don't care that I have been homeless and my career and my dreams all went down in flames. They have love to give and they can only give it by being held. They can only receive our love by the same method. Babies must be touched...and then they touch us. Babies scare no one. Babies do not intimidate. Babies have no history, and we have no history with them.

L'enchante understood this and he received the greatest gift on this special night. He instinctively knew that this child only wanted one thing...to love this shepherd.

The shepherd cast aside his pretense and his fear and got lost in the wonder...as his name implies, he was "enchanted" with this baby. He came with nothing...he left with the greatest gift of all.

He is shipwrecked in his bliss, at the stable of his Affection.

Perhaps this one scene would serve best as a model for me at Christmas. I have to come to understand that I need bring nothing to this place. This baby desires no gifts or acts of service. He only desires my heart. He longs for me to sit quietly and rock him in my arms and let Him pour his wondrous love on my aching and wounded soul. He loves it when I have my epiphany moment when I am holding him and it hits me... "This is *God*! He came here like this for *me*! He did this so I could get this close to Him"

L'Enchante understood that truth very early on in his experience with this baby and he sets the standard for us as we approach this infant-king. L'Enchante is a true ragamuffin who knows that this baby came for ragamuffins most of all.

*Note: This is my version of the tale of L'enchante. The story of L'enchante is still told in the forests of Provence, France. It's tradition is part of a small hamlet with a dying culture. I first read the tale in Lion and Lamb; The Relentless Tenderness of Jesus" by Brennan Manning. I will be forever grateful for learning this wonderful little story.

December 10

Mi Padre

There is an overwhelming feeling of sadness before I even open the little leather door on the calendar today. In the days that have preceded this one, I have yet to have the feeling that I knew what was coming next or what scene I would bear witness to when I folded back the leather door and peered inside, and found myself interacting with the characters.

But this morning is different. For no apparent reason, I have the heavy feeling that I already know that whatever I see behind this door will not be pleasant for me. That it will perhaps be unsettling or sorrowful. Many of the scenes have been difficult, but they have almost always, without exception, ended in hope.

I open the door and I am instantly seated in the corner of the cave across from Mary and Joseph. They are looking at me with great sadness in their eyes. Mary is crying and Joseph is caught between bewilderment and disdain. I can see that they both want to come to my side but they also sense that I need to observe this myself and make my peace with our visitor.

I don't hesitate. I don't have to rub my eyes or squint in the flickering light of the oil lamps. I don't have to jog my memory or try to recall a name. I know instantly who this guest is. *It's my dad.*

I have only ever met my father one time. We have no relationship and it is a pain I bear and will bear for all my days. I have accepted it and I don't let it destroy me but it hurts nonetheless.

My dad is a great man. He is a great success and a war hero and a very well educated man. He is a husband and a devoted father to two other children. He was a college athlete and has led an exemplary and heroic life. He is the man I still hope I can become someday. But he desires no relationship with me and I have wrestled with this truth for 26 years now.

I am seated behind him, about 10 feet away hidden in the shadows. I am certain he can't see me and I prefer the anonymity. Where other visitors have had much to say to Jesus during their interaction with the baby-king, my dad is silent.

I can see his face from the side and he is enraptured with this child, holding him like he would his own son. My father is an introspective man and he is studying Jesus' face with the loving look of a dad. There is adoration in his eyes and wonder in his slight smile.

I see myself in his face. I have heard myself on those few occasions when we spoke. I have looked for the slightest sign of approval or connection over the years but those things are phantoms that dart and weave but never stand still long enough to be attained.

But here tonight, in a dirty cave, my dad is holding this little baby the way he might have held me when I was born…had he had the opportunity. There is delight in his eyes and love in his gentleness. I wish I was this baby. I wish I could have known my father's touch just one time. It is too late for that now. I am 47 and my dad approaches 70. The time for tenderness between a father and his child had long since passed.

But for a long time I see the way this baby is smiling, and absorbing the affections that I never knew, and I am a tumultuous collision of jealousy, envy, anger, and sadness. I wish this could have been me. Maybe things would have been different. Maybe there could have been something more to this life if my dad had only been there that night in September 1963. Maybe if he had been allowed a role in my life as I grew up…

The tortured thoughts roll around in my head for a long time as I watch my father loving a child of the same questionable background as his own firstborn son. Not a sound is made. Not a word is uttered. Jesus is strangely silent. Mary and Joseph say nothing, choosing to observe the scene in sorrow and sadness. And I— despite the volcano erupting in my soul—have no way to connect the thoughts raging in my heart to the words in my mind. There is simply nothing to say here.

I want to run over to him and throw my arms around him and hug my dad. I want to hear him tell me he loves me for the first time in my life. I want to know what it would have been like had he ever held me this way the night I entered this world. I find a strange emotional response rising within my heart. I am now looking at Jesus more so than my father.

He is God…granted He is in a tiny body only hours old, but He is God in human form. And my father is holding him when he never held me. He is offering Him love that I never knew…and likely never will. How can Jesus abide this? Can't he fuss just a little bit and validate the seeming injustice being done? Couldn't he spit-up on my dad's shirt just as a way of saying "there…that's what I think of your worship!" Can nothing ever change this picture?

Then I see Jesus smiling slightly at my dad. And I recall that while my earthly father, for reasons of his own, might not have been able to give me his love, my Heavenly Father…the father of this tiny baby I am watching my dad gently nestle and love on…has always offered me the love I seek.

Jesus becomes a son to my dad each year at Christmas. Each year, as he worships this baby during advent, he offers his love to a baby boy who was born illegitimate. And every single day, this baby's Father loves me more than even my own father ever could, even if the situation had been perfect from the beginning. The boy comes to connect us both somehow. Because the boy came to my dad, (and all of us) I can go to his Father to find the dad I have always needed.

God so frequently desires us to refer to Him as "Father", "Abba", and "Papa". He longs to be the Father we have so desperately sought. But first He had to come as the Son we all long to be. The beloved son that our father adores without question and without limit or condition.

And as I watch Jesus look lovingly on my dad when I expected him to be disruptive or disagreeable, I understand the lesson here. Jesus loves my dad...more than I do even. Jesus holds nothing against him, not even the failed connection between us. Because after all...we are both ragamuffins here at this cave, both shipwrecks built in the same shipyard. Jesus loves my dad, and so I must love him this way as well

...and I do

December 11

The Legalist

It is a cold, rainy, late fall day in Philadelphia. It is typical for early December; damp and gray. I still haven't gotten into the spirit of the season and it is worrying me, but Christmas rushes toward us regardless. Another day dawns and another opportunity to see what further mysteries the little advent calendar holds.

I open the little leather door. For the first time in 8 days, I don't like the image I see. It is an older man, I don't know him, yet he seems familiar. I decide to stand to the side and observe. He arrives at the cave with trepidation.

My heart tells me he has made this journey many times in the past and it has always left him discomfited. This place ruins his theology every time he comes here. Yet he comes back each year because he so desperately wants what this baby offers. He just can't get used to the surroundings and the poverty and the dirt.

The overflowing love of an infant Savior makes him uneasy. He has never been comfortable merely accepting this child as he is. This man has always thought God was too easy on us all and that we need to strain more to accept this gift. (The true nature of a gift being lost on his tired soul long ago)

So again he comes, trying to find a way to reconcile this place and this child with his legalistic theology. He huffs and puffs around the entrance to the cave until finally he bows and scurries in, like a chipmunk running for the hollow of a fallen oak.

He crawls in on hands and knees, making a mental note of how well dressed he is compared to Mary and Joseph and the other visitors. Then he sees how filthy everything is, and that much of that filth is getting his brand new charcoal suit dirty. He is flustered now because he didn't plan on getting dirty...and this a new suit.

He looks around, grasps Josephs hand heartily, and nods toward Mary as if she had recently broken wind and the smell was still lingering. Mary smiles gently and thinks to herself how every time he comes here he behaves the same way towards her. "One of these days..." Mary says beneath a cunning smile, "...I will go give him a hug and tell him 'You do realize I am not Catholic?" This makes Mary giggle a little... she is still a teenager after all.

The man glances around at the unbelievably dismal surroundings and he gives a shudder. "This is wrong" he thinks to himself. "This scene is wrong somehow. This poverty, this humbleness. He is a King for God's sake!"

He glances at his watch, "Good I am early...the wise men haven't even arrived yet" he thinks this every year, and prides himself on getting here ahead of the much ballyhooed Orient Kings. This man is approaching 80 years old and still doesn't realize that they won't be coming tonight. Joseph tried explaining that to him once when he asked, but the old man argued with him so vehemently that he gave up trying. Joseph and Mary tolerate this man for one reason only...and I am about to find out why.

The old man looks at the four figures around the manger in annoyance. They have been there since he arrived and he is late. He has a candle light service to attend and now he is going to have to change suits before he can go. Besides, these men are shepherds and they are really smelly.

Three of them are standing, albeit hunched over and one man is on his knees rocking slowly back and forth. The three are speaking to him, trying to get him to finish up and get going.

"L'enchante...L'enchante, we must be leaving! "But the fourth shepherd is lost in adoration and the only response they get is his melodic, whispered worship tune..."Jesu...Jesu..." His tears flow freely and his smile is as nothing anyone has ever seen. The old man clears his throat loudly and taps on his watch when one of the shepherds looks back.

They have no idea what the gesture means, having never seen a watch, but they assume he is in a hurry. The shepherd blushes and finally the fourth man rises to his hunched over position with his three compatriots. They walk past the old man apologetically and he offers a bleak, pained smile.

Now he is alone with the child. He crouches down so as not to kneel, not wanting to further soil his new charcoal suit. He arrives at the manger and for a moment, he seems to soften. A few tears come to his eyes but he resists them. He looks at the tiny figure stirring in the crib and his heart aches to hold him. His hand reaches for a tiny finger but withdraws instantly. "No!" he thinks..."This is the Savior...he cannot be touched!"

His hands tremble and his heart is on fire in his chest. Being this close to that which he adores and still not reaching out to him and holding him...his god-nature cries out "Pick Him up!" but his legalistic flesh refuses. "Never!" he says to himself..."This is sacred and holy...I cannot touch him nor can He touch me. I would die."

The conflict is visible and the baby begins to cry, perhaps because of the turmoil in the mans heart and on his face. The baby is reaching a tiny hand toward this man and the mans heart is wrenched.

Mary can stand no more of this and she rushes to her son. She turns a fiery glance at the old man and spits out; "Every time you come here, my son longs for you to pick him up and hold him. And you always refuse. Why? Why do you not understand that a baby must be held to give it's love and to receive yours? Why do you not understand this?!"

Mary blushes as she realizes she is raising her voice at this man. But her mother's heart is wounded because of this man's rejection of her son's loving overtures, yet she shows compassion to him.

"Sir" she whispers as her tiny hand touches his, "I can see that you have love for him...but he is a baby and he cannot take that love you bring unless you touch him. And he cannot love you in return unless you let him touch you."

The old man trembles and almost breaks. Everything in his old soul longs to hold this child. He knows he has the very son of God...his own savior...right here and he could touch Him, but he refuses.

He has all that he has ever longed for at his disposal, but his pride, and the depth of his legalism prevent him and he stumbles out of the cave yet again...untouched and unchanged refusing to be shipwrecked and not understanding how very shipwrecked he really is.

December 12

"Peanuts"

This morning I am busier than I have ever been and I almost forget to open the door on the little calendar. I pause, looking over doors already opened. Only 12 left...we are more than halfway there. How does this go by so quickly? I open the door for today and instantly recognize the face. Not everyone would know this man to see him but they know his work.

I was always a huge fan so I know the man behind the characters. He kneels by the manger in prayer and has one hand inside, touching the baby. The baby is as enchanted with this man as the man is with Him. Perhaps it is the spirit of the man in communion with his Savior. Or maybe the child just finds him as amusing as millions of others did.

The man is smiling and content. He looks at the child lovingly and speaks softly.

"Jesus", he whispers, *"I am so privileged to be here with you. You make me happy. I tried to use my job to bring that happiness to others and I tried to reveal you in my work. It wasn't the kind of work that most people would think of as evangelistic or even "Christian" but I kept getting letters from people who found You in what I did. I am so thankful for having known You all those years and for having the chance to share you with the world...in my way."* The man smiles and whispers...more to himself than the baby... *"So many children...so many people...looking back on it, it was so easy to show them this baby. He was in every frame...every conversation"*

The man perks up a bit and looks at the child once more, "You know the special I drew up for you at Christmas? 45 years and they still play it on national TV...and they still have Linus telling your story word for word...as crazy as things have gotten they haven't taken that out yet."

The baby smiles at the man, as most of us have in our lives. The man is Charles Schulz, creator of "Peanuts" and the wonderful "Charlie Brown Christmas" that has been on national TV since 1964 and still contains a verbatim presentation of the story of Christ's nativity. Schulz, who passed away in 2000, was a devout Christian man who incorporated Jesus into his work until the very end. We may never know how many millions of people learned simple truths about God from the colorful frames in Sunday morning funny papers...or when Linus took center stage and said "Lights please..." and told us of the Nativity.

Tonight, Charles Schulz is a shipwreck at the very manger he so wonderfully drew us to as children. Proof that if you lay your gifts at the feet of this tiny infant-king, He will bless them in ways you cannot even dream. He uses even shipwrecks to guide other shipwrecks here.

December 13

Christmas on the Block

I stirred suddenly at the sound of the bells from the church and I realize that I have been smiling broadly. Yesterday's scene really brought me happiness. Charles Schulz was a hero of mine and I loved his work. It was good to see his love for the savior.

Taking the calendar in my hands I hesitate before opening the next scene. I examine the calendar again, half way through now and I am truly understanding the mystery and wonder that my friend Wick was hoping I would find...and I think he knew all along I would.

I open the little door and I recognize the faces. Instantly a song runs through my mind. It's one of my favorite Christmas songs, by a Philadelphia artist named Allan Mann.

The song is called "Christmas on the Block"

There's a Streetlight that sits above the night
And it shines its gray light on the midnight air
And the houses twinkle on the block
But there's one house that shines a special way out there

And it's Christmas in the city
And the trees are lighted pretty
But the prettiest Christmas Tree of all
Can you see all the colors that we cannot?
And theirs is the most beautiful
Christmas on the Block

Though they cannot see the light of day
And the night is forever, the fact still remains
In this world of confusion there is peace
There is hope and despair, sometimes the beauty is a beast
And they cannot see the lightning
And they cannot see the thunder

But they know what no one understands
That beauty is a blessing; love is all we've got
And theirs is the most beautiful
Christmas on the block

In the darkest corner of the night
Only dreams illuminate their eyes
And they see all the colors
That we cannot
And theirs is the most beautiful
Christmas on the block

And they cannot see the lightning
And they cannot see the thunder
But they know what no one understands

That beauty is a blessing
Love is all we've got
And theirs is the most beautiful
Christmas on the block

Two figures enter the cave with the unmistakable hesitancy of blindness. The couple bows and slowly makes their way to the manger. Mary is moved to tears with compassion for the blind couple who have come to worship their Savior. Each year, it is their arrival that moves Mary and Joseph the most. They have such love for the child and yet they have never gazed on His face with earthly eyes.

They have been blind from birth and they have never seen any baby, much less the infant Son of God.

They find their way to the side of the crib, and they reach in to pick Him up. Mary smiles through tears of joy and Joseph looks on with admiration. They have said nothing to each other until now. "Hello Mary...hello Joseph" the couple whisper. Mary chokes back tears. Their voices sound like the familiar sounds of old friends.

Maybe it is because this couple, who needs so much from this Savior, has never asked for anything. They have not only accepted their blindness, but used it to bless others who have perfect physical sight. They don't complain, they don't whine. They decorate a tree on their front porch and invite people from the entire city to come and decorate it with them. In doing so they share Jesus with the city.

They know how to hold Christmas in their hearts and it just naturally overflows onto the streets of Upper Darby, the neighborhood in Philadelphia where they live in a modest row home, and on to the rest of my hometown.

They never considered when they began their tradition, that a young and talented songwriter would write a Christmas song about them and it would wind up on MTV in the early budding days of the network. They just wanted to show the world that they *got it*. That they knew that Christmas was more than things you can see.

Mary hugs the woman a long time. They are practically friends and Mary seems somehow comfortable with her in a way the other visitors don't leave her feeling. Perhaps it is the blindness, or the simplicity. Likely it is the fact that this wonderful blind couple comes here each year and never asks for anything from the baby. They just spend time loving Him.

The woman holds Jesus affectionately and traces His face delicately with her fingertips. "He is so beautiful!" is her hushed whisper. Her husband fumbles for her hand and says "Show me..." The woman takes his hand in hers and together they gently touch Jesus cheeks, His lips, they stroke His hair. He is enamored with this couple. They ask for nothing. They are as vulnerable in their blindness as He is in His infancy. He somehow knows this and it makes him smile.

Mary whispers in the darkness to the couple, "If you asked Him, I believe he would, even at this age." The woman smiles in the direction of her voice, "Oh no Mary. God must have wanted us this way for a reason. We don't need to be healed to love Him "I know that" Mary smiles, "But I bet He would anyway".

The couple worships Jesus for a long long time. They touch His face and commit His features to memory. He falls asleep in her arms and she places Him in his manger crib.

The husband and wife turn and crawl towards the doorway. They stop and Mary and Joseph hug them for unashamedly for several minutes. You are our most welcome guests" Mary says "Thank you for loving my son". The man wipes tears away and smiles. "Mary...Joseph...thank you for letting us see Him. When we close our eyes in worship, we see Him just as clearly as everyone else does." Mary weeps openly at these words. Joseph hugs the man for a long time. "We have to go," the wife whispers to Mary, "There are a few more lights to put on that tree on our porch and people will be stopping by until late into the night."

The blind couple fumble in their perpetual darkness toward the cave entrance and out into the night...heading home to the Upper Darby section of Philadelphia, to finish their tree that tells the real story of Christmas.

They are shipwrecked at a stable they have never seen...except in their hearts where it matters most.

Here is a link to the video for this beautiful and moving song

http://www.youtube.com/watch?v=5zCaUeiuSx0

December 14

The Roman

I will admit I am tired. I awoke at 3:40 this morning, tried to go back to sleep and finally surrendered to the morning at 4:30. I don't mind getting up early, but this whole week has worn me out emotionally and I need to recharge somehow.

I open the leather door on the calendar and there is a man standing there in full battle armament. I have no idea who this is. He is wearing a metal chest piece, a shield, spiked shoes, and a helmet and is carrying a spear and has a sword slung at his side. He is a fearsome man to behold. He is pacing frantically outside the doorway to the cave and he appears frustrated.

When he walks off about 20 feet, I crawl inside and find Joseph sitting cross legged in the straw. Mary is holding Jesus...rocking Him to sleep after nursing him. "Who is this man?" I ask Joseph. "A Roman soldier." Joseph answers. "He really wants to come in but he has seen inside this cave and he knows he has to take all that armor off just to get through the doorway. He is on duty...technically at least...and he isn't allowed to do that until his watch is over."

Joseph and I watch the large, menacing figure stalking back and forth outside the cave for a good 15 minutes. At some point Mary has placed Jesus in His manger and has joined us in watching this scene. She leans her tiny head on Joseph's chest and he strokes her dark hair. "Do you think he'll come in?" she whispers. "I hope so", Joseph replies,

"He is so distraught. If he wants to see him, he should just come in and do it." Mary frowns a little, "Has he said anything to you?" "Earlier, when he first got here, he asked me if I could bring Him out to see him." Joseph says, "I told him that was impossible. If he wants to come see Him he is very welcome but he has to come inside the cave."

After a long while, the man outside heaves a heavy sigh. He walks to the cave doorway and squats down. He is a large man, about my size (I am 6' 4") and he seems amused to see the three of us watching his antics from inside the cave. "Is it still okay?" he booms. "Ssshhhhh!" The three of us answer him simultaneously, and then look at each other with a grin. Joseph answers him, "Certainly...come inside."

The man stands up and looks around nervously. Then he begins to remove his armor. He unbuckles his sheathed sword and props it against the wall of the cave. He removes his chest plate and his coat of mail beneath. He takes off his helmet and his leather and spike wrist wraps that go all the way to his elbows. He removes the heavy, spiked boots on his feet and replaces them with a pair of leather sandals from his backpack and comes into the tent on his hands and knees.

He looks extremely uncomfortable as he crawls over to the three of us. He looks at me especially with a sort of amusement. Seeing another man his size, crammed into such a small space must seem cartoonish to him. Mary touches his hand lightly and he quickly withdraws his arm. Mary is slightly startled but with all the wonder she has seen on this night, little surprises her anymore.

"He is right over here, sir" Mary leads the man to where the sleeping Jesus lay in his feed-trough crib. The man is suddenly reduced to childlike wonder. He smiles and looks at the little boy with a gentle face. He has transformed from a rough and tumble Roman soldier to a gentle man. His eyes sparkle and his body language speaks of great affection. Mary whispers to him, "Would you like to hold Him?" The man looks at

Mary startled, with a quizzical look on his face. "Oh no Mary...I mean I would love to but I couldn't. It wouldn't be right." Mary smiles gently and asks, "Why not?"

The man looks at the ground and sadness crosses his face. "Because I am a man of war...a Roman soldier. I have done horrible things in my past and I have blood on my hands." At this the large man holds up his hands in the oil-lamp light and shows Mary the crimson stains that he has never been able to wash clean. "It's permanent" he says, "I have tried every soap known to man, but these stains won't wash off."

Mary touches his hands gently; her eyes run over the red skin that extends from his fingers to his elbows. "And now?" Mary asks, the Roman replies; "I gained enough rank to transfer to a guard position. I don't see battle and bloodshed anymore, but I am still a Roman soldier and I still have this blood on my hands that won't wash off. I don't think its right to touch a baby with these hands of mine not this baby especially."

Mary smiles and a tear falls softly on her robe. "Sir," she whispers, "I am only just now starting to understand much about my son. I know he is here for a purpose. I am not exactly sure what it is, but something in my spirit tells me he would not mind your stained hands." The man chokes back tears and there is a look in his eyes of pity for Mary, like he might know something she doesn't and it isn't good. "You are more right than you know Mary...do you really think it would be okay?"

Mary nods and smiles, "Yes of course". She reaches into the crib and lifts Jesus tenderly and places

Him in the mans huge arms. The man trembles. Tears fall on the little cloth blanket with the letters "D.D.O.C" on it.

The man whispers to Jesus, "I know who you are. I know why you are here. I saw you that day and I am so sorry...so sorry for what we did to you..." the man breaks down into stifled sobs. Even here...in this moment, he is still thinking like a soldier and blocking emotion. "I saw you then...I wanted to come and see you here...now" the man continues, "Before that moment. Before that awful, terrible moment. And I wanted to thank you, because you changed me. I had to keep it a secret, but you changed me."

The baby stirs and moves slightly and yawns and continues His slumber. Mary smiles and touches the man's shoulder, "He likes you" she says. Those simple words break the last vestige of toughness in this man's heart. He breaks into silent sobs, holding his tongue as best he can. He pulls Jesus close to his chest and tells Him, "I love you". He turns and hands Jesus to Mary. She takes her little son into her arms and suddenly she lets out a small frail gasp. "Sir!" she whispers, "Your arms...your hands!"

The enormous Roman soldier moves his hands into the light of the oil lamp and he is in shocked amazement. The crimson is gone. His skin is as white as the newborn baby's he just held. He turns his hands over in the light and cannot find a trace of red bloodstain anywhere. The man smiles a disbelieving smile and impulsively throws his arms around Mary and Jesus in a gentle bear hug. "Surely this is the Son of God!" the man says.

Then it hits me...I know who he is! He is the Roman soldier who stood by and watched as Jesus died on the cross. When the earth quaked and the veil tore and the graves blew open...this man recognized Jesus for who He really was. He has come to see Him as a child this time, to complete his encounter. The red stains are gone and the change is complete.

He is suddenly softer and more gentle. He looks at his hands over and over with a smile that defies description. He embraces Mary and Joseph, nods at me with a grin, and crawls out the doorway and walks off into the distance, looking at his snow white hands.

He leaves behind his armor at the doorway of the cave, he is a man of peace, at peace with the tiny Prince of Peace, and he leaves the armor as a testimony. A reminder that a shipwreck has been to this stable and has surely seen the Son of God.

December 15

The Lost

So many scenes have left their imprint on my soul this Advent season. Wick was right...this is a very special calendar. My chair is soft and comfortable and I have clearly lost track of time today. I miss Morgan. I wish she was experiencing this calendar with me. But then maybe this would be a lot for a 12 year old to comprehend.

I open the little door and a chill runs through me...it's not from the temperature outside. The scene behind the door is a view from inside the cave, looking out. The night is clear and cold; much like last night was, here in Philadelphia. I peer through the low passageway and Mary and Joseph are behind me looking out as well.

There is a commotion outside and a huge crowd of angry, disoriented, unhappy people. They are moving toward the cave in desperation and almost as soon as they are near enough to have to lower their heads to enter, a brilliant white light appears. The light is so bright it seems like the sun and it is blinding in its intensity.

I have a better view because I am inside and much of this light is blocked by the low doorway. I can make out an enormous man now standing in front of the door. The light is emanating from him and he is blocking the entrance so that none of these people outside can come in.

Mary walks away sadly and Joseph leans over and whispers, "Maybe you'd better come away from the door...you don't really want to see this." I want to heed his advice, after all he knows what is going on, but something makes me watch.

Because the angel is in front of me and the doorway blocks most of the glare, I have a pretty good view of what is happening outside. However the people out there who are trying to get in are nearly blinded without shielding their eyes or looking away altogether.

But they are determined to gain entrance. One by one they walk up to the angel and attempt to persuade him to allow them to come inside.

The first man seems to be an important fellow. He is dressed in what looks like the clothing the Romans wore back in Jesus' time. He begins pleading with the angel at the doorway "You must let me see Him! You must! I have to see Him!" He repeats his pleading over and over but the angel has no reply and only shakes his head.

The man draws nearer to the angel and falls at his feet. Then I know who this is! His hands are rubbed raw and bleeding and he is still rubbing them continuously ...as if washing them. He is screaming now "But I find no fault in Him...I find no fault in Him...No fault in Him...Please! I must see Him. I find no fault in Him!" It is Pontius Pilate. I am shaking as I watch his pitiful display.

The angel remains resolute against the desperate pleas of this Roman governor who thought he could simply wash his hands of the guilt of Christ's death all those years ago. He was wrong and an eternity of damnation has never removed that guilt or the desperate desire to have that moment all over again. But that opportunity is gone. The baby-savior will not receive this guest tonight.

Pilate finally accepts the futility of his situation and turns and walks off into the night to return to his eternal separation from this child. As soon as he has gone, a near riot ensues for his spot in line...there is absolutely no love nor grace to be found in this crowd...and a regal-looking man with a singed and tarnished crown falls at the feet of the angel guarding the doorway. He has his wife with him, but there is not a shred of affection perceivable between them. He is grasping at the sandals of the angel and begging to gain entrance to see Jesus, but the angel says "Almost is not good enough!"

The angels voice booms like thunder and I feel the ground shake at the reverberation. The kingly man looks up in tears and says "Wait...Paul! I know Paul! Send for Paul! Paul can get me in...Paul spoke with me about this child...Paul knows me angel! Paul knows me!" The angel frowns and repeats his command... "Almost is not enough, Agrippa...you had your chance long ago. You will not have another. Away with you!"

The once great King Agrippa turns and walks into the outer darkness and back to his eternal horror, once again having come close to Jesus but not close enough. He walks away without being forced because hell, as heaven is a matter of choosing, and Agrippa knows this now.

All night this continues...I want to turn my head but I find myself watching the sad hopeless parade. Voltaire, Stalin, Genghis Khan, Marx...small and great they come and one by one they find no access to the wonderful hope that sleeps in this dirty hovel.

Business men and power brokers. Athletes and dignitaries. Housewives and homeless. All had their chance in life in some form or fashion, but all of these folks chose not to choose Him. It is a seemingly endless train of devastation. In life they rejected Jesus and thought they didn't need Him. In death, they desperately realize how they need Him and part of their eternal punishment is that knowing and that longing and that desperation.

They are forever locked in a place where not a shred of Jesus' grace or Presence can penetrate. That is the worst part of all their torture; they are in the one place where the love of God will not reach. There is no one more lost than these souls.

They are shipwrecked but the stable which once beckoned to them clearly, now has no room for them.

December 16

Reconciled and Redeemed... by a Baby

Sometime before 5 AM the church bells woke me up and I realized I was trapped in that terrible overlapping land where it is too early to get up but too late to go back to sleep. It's the purgatory of slumber I suppose, like being in the middle of a great dream and realizing... "This is a dream". That's where I was this morning when the bells clanged their mournful song.

There wasn't any sense in trying to sleep for 30 more minutes, so I decide to just get up and maybe spend some time in contemplation and thought. I need to figure out where Christmas went. I plop down in my big chair and pick up the beautiful hand-made calendar and open the leather trimmed door for day 17. I have no idea at all who the figure is I see.

Mary and Joseph are standing to the side of the manger and there is gentle love in their eyes. A black man with an athletic build is kneeling by the crib with his back toward me. He is holding the baby in his large powerful arms, dwarfing the tiny figure. The man is very happy and seems to be soaking in the love from the child's radiant face. The baby is smiling noticeably at the man and the man is weeping openly. I hear him speaking softly to the baby "Thank You Jesus...thank you Jesus...Thank you for forgiveness...thank you for redeeming me...oh thank you Lord..."

The man rocks the child for a long time. For one brief second he raises his head and I recognize the handsome face of a man from back home. His name is Andre Deputy. I never knew Andre, but a friend of mine, Bill Killen, was his liaison and worked on his behalf to try to get him a pardon.

Because Andre Deputy is a murderer...

On February 1, 1979, in a drunken stupor, he and another man murdered an elderly couple in a botched robbery. They were trying to get more money for booze, and things went crazy and a man and his wife were murdered violently.

Sometime during his years in prison, Andre found himself shipwrecked at this stable and fell down before this same infant-Savior. He offered the baby the ultimate gift...his soul. He did the most loving thing anyone can do for Jesus...he let Jesus love him.

The remainder of Andre's life was spent serving his fellow prisoners. He got his GED, completed a correspondence Bible course and taught bible studies to inmates. He was instrumental in leading dozens of other inmates to this Savior he now kneels before.

At his commutation hearing, a quadriplegic inmate who had been paralyzed in a gang fight in prison had himself wheeled into the board room. With tears in his eyes he recounted how Andre' would wake up early and come into this mans room after head count and help him get cleaned up and dressed. Then he would wheel him into the chow line and make sure he got his food.

After breakfast Andre' would return the man to his cell and they would have a bible study and prayer together. Andre did his laundry for him, he wrote letters for him. He even brushed the mans' teeth. The man was sobbing inconsolably as he told the pardon board how "Andre is my friend...if you take him from me I don't know how I'll make it".

My friend Bill told me this story through tears of his own. Andre's encounter with this infant King was real and life changing, as all real redemption is. Andre' Deputy was a legend for Jesus in the Smyrna Correctional Facility.

I watch in earnest now that I know who this man is. I see him holding Jesus closely and I see how clear and bright his eyes are. No alcoholic fog, no guilt and shame...the love of the infant is radiating back to him as he pours out his affection on his baby-King.

There is a stirring near the entrance and Mary and Joseph look toward the doorway. They smile broadly and silently motion the visitors to join them. They walk to Mary and Joseph and they whisper greetings. The couple seems happy and content and the woman places a finger on her lips. " Shhhh" she whispers to Mary. Mary's tears tell the story and Joseph is blinking back some of his own.

At the manger, Andre Deputy is lost in worship and gently holding Jesus to his chest. His eyes are closed and he is unaware that the old couple has knelt down beside him. The man and woman place a hand on each of Andre's strong shoulders and he smiles without opening his eyes. "I think he is asleep Mary", Andre whispers.

The old woman squeezes his shoulder and her voice breaks..."Andre'..." Andre opens his eyes with a start. His face wears a sudden shocked and pained look. The old couple is Byard and Alberta Smith...the elderly couple he killed while robbing them 30 years ago.

Andre is frightened and gently places Jesus in his cradle. He wants to speak but is afraid. The old man realizes he will have to break the ice. "André...son...it's okay. We have come here every year since, hoping to find you. We heard about your accepting Jesus, the angels rejoiced, son. We rejoiced too. We finally found you here...we came to worship Him with you..."

Andre Deputy breaks down. His sobs are louder than anything I have heard thus far, but for all the tears there is a palpable joy in his crying. The Smiths are embracing him to the point of holding him up. Andre looks at the infant baby in the manger and sees the smile on the boy's lips. He reaches into a mesh bag he has brought with him to the cave. It is the kind of bag inmates use to transport their purchases from the commissary to their cells. He pulls out a small piece of fabric. It is ragged on the edges, like it has been torn.

As Andre shakes the piece of fabric open and gently lays it over the tiny child, I can make out the letters, "D.D.O.C."... *Delaware Department of Corrections.*

Deputy leans over to kiss the infant and whispers, "Here little baby...I am free now. I have a beautiful white robe thanks to you. Maybe this can keep you warm." Jesus has exchanged a robe for the ragged piece of a prison garment and it leaves Andre Deputy free and forgiven.

The Smiths and their murderer are joined together in worship, forgiveness, and reconciliation, around the only One who could possibly redeem a situation like this. They are shipwrecked together and redeemed at the stable. By the conquering love of a poor baby-savior.

"Redemption rips through the surface of time...in the cry of a tiny babe"

Authors note Andre Deputy was put to death by lethal injection, June 24, 1994

December 17

The Fisherman

The smell of snow is in the air today. For the first time since I was a baby, the Delaware Valley has a serious chance for a white Christmas.

I glance at yesterday's open door and see the blanket made from a prison jumpsuit and then I see the pile of armor and weapons left outside the cave.

Yesterday's advent was special. Today I open the little door and there is a scene that I was not expecting.

A man lies on the ground in front of the cave. He is unconscious and bleeding from his head. Mary and Joseph are trying to stop the bleeding and wake him up. I hand Mary a scrap of cloth and ask what happened.

"He was in such a hurry to come in and see Him, that he didn't bow low enough and he hit his head on the ledge." Was Mary's reply. "He is a very impulsive man and this isn't unusual for him." Joseph snickers and grins, "Mary is being kind right now..." Joseph laughs, "This man is pretty reckless and uncouth. I am surprised he has lived this long."

The man stirs and sits up slowly. He seems familiar but I haven't placed him yet. Joseph looks at me and before he opens his mouth, I tell him, No...Let me try to figure it out first." Joseph laughs at this and says, "It will come to you quickly!"

The man is embarrassed by his accident and fumbling for words. I'm sorry...I was in a hurry...and he is here and I need to see Him...I didn't duck and...He is here! I need to see Him now!" The man's words are scatter-shot and almost nonsensical. Probably because he is in such a hurry and filled with such passion for this child. That passion marks his every move it seems.

He bows and enters the cave, almost ignoring Joseph and Mary. He crawls through the muddy straw on the floor with no regard for the stains it leaves in his clothing. His love for the Child is genuine, that's for sure, he was crying before he even got near the manger. He doesn't ask anyone, he instantly reaches into the crib and lifts Jesus in his arms. Jesus isn't startled, but appears mildly annoyed with this impulsive man. Still...there is love abounding in the baby's eyes.

The man cradles the boy and smiles. "There you are...there you are my Lord!" he says, in a voice much louder than he realizes. This is not a man prone to whispering and it is a skill he hasn't quite mastered. The man begins telling the baby about things that are happening in his life. Churches he has helped to start, people he has introduced to the Savior, hardships he has endured. After a lengthy recitation of his deeds, the man grows quiet. Quiet and thoughtful.

It is a long silence after such a tremendous outpouring and it reminds me that within all of us there are caverns and sections of our heart which hold deep truth and amazing perspective. If I would judge this man on the first five minutes that I have seen here, I would have been sadly mistaken and missed the best part of his soul. The man is smiling now...and silent. His eyes fill with tears and he seems very happy.

"What times we had...especially in those early days" he says to the baby, "That day I met you, and I was mending nets and my clothes smelled like bait! You were still so respectful of me and so kind..." With that I realize who he is...it is Peter. Peter the impulsive disciple. Peter continues, "That wedding feast...that was fun. That was before the spotlight was on You and we had a good time as friends enjoying each others company. The blind man...when you spit on the ground and put mud on his eyes..!" Peter bellows at this one, "Those Pharisees were so baffled! Mud! That was great!" I thought Peter's loud boisterous laughter would startle the baby, but he smiled and let out a little coo. I guess he was laughing along.

Peter grew sullen again...and sad. He looked Jesus in the eyes for a long and quiet few moments. "I still get embarrassed about jumping out of that boat...and for wanting to build the tabernacles for Elijah and Moses and You...sometimes I should keep my mouth shut."

Before those words have echoed off the cave walls, Peter clutches Jesus to his neck and whispers, "I am so sorry about that night...with those soldiers and that servant girl. I was scared, I was confused. They were hurting you and I couldn't make them stop and I got angry"

Peter is trying to avoid tears as he continues, "Before I knew it, I was denying You. It was like the words just shot out of me..." I am transfixed at this scene and don't realize Joseph coming over to me. "Go to him," Joseph says, "What?!" I ask, quite baffled, "I thought I couldn't interfere..." "This one is different, I think" Joseph answers.

I am mystified...approaching a disciple...a church father. I pause a long time and finally I hear Peter say, "Come here son, I want to see you". I am stunned. I love this man. I find so much of myself in him. He is reckless, impulsive, outgoing, boisterous, bold, brash, and intelligent.

He is fearless and fearful at once. He has let his heart overrule his senses and the result has shot out of his mouth on many occasions. Yet he loved Jesus so fiercely that when the time came and he was to be crucified, he asked that they do it in a different fashion because he didn't feel worthy to die in the same manner as his Lord.

He could have been my father.

I approach the patriarch of my faith with trepidation. This is *Peter*. I kneel next to him and he pauses a long time. Finally he speaks,

"See how loving He is?" He asks me, *"That has never changed. I jumped out of a boat and then nearly drowned. I interrupted a miracle on the mountain top with my own desire to do something great for Him that wasn't necessary. I chopped off a young kid's ear in a flight of rage. I betrayed this baby in front of God and men on the night He needed my friendship the most."* Peter pauses here and chokes back tears. *"...and all He ever did was love me anyway and practically beg me to take care of his children for Him. 'Feed my lambs' He said to me on the beach that day. None of my failures or frailties mattered to Him. Just my love and my willingness. That's what He wants from you too, son. You and I have the same personality. You love Him fiercely...you love everyone fiercely if you love them at all. That can get you into trouble sometimes but it can also be the most wonderful love there is. You can't give*

away love if you are holding some of it back. That includes your love for Him. You can't measure it out and you can't do it in any other way except that way He created you to. Love Him your way. Let Him love you! Be who He created you to be with no apologies! You are not obligated to perfection any more than anyone else is and nobody has the right to throw that yoke of bondage on you. My friends were a ragtag bunch, but they never threw my denial of Him in my face. They understood that he is shaping me every day of my life and today's story is not who I am...it's just who I am today. Remember that."

With that, Peter handed Jesus to me and crawled out of the cave without looking back. Mary came over and took Jesus from my arms and placed Him in the manger. Joseph smiled and said, "Peter looked very happy as he left..."

December 18

Revelation

In a day I have dreamed about since I was a child, we are getting hammered with the largest pre-Christmas snowfall I can remember. Possibly 20 inches will fall by tomorrow morning. Hopefully the temps will stay low and it will remain for Christmas.

I open the advent calendar door and there is an enormous line stretching off into the distance, leading up to the cave. I don't need any introduction from Mary or Joseph...they are smiling in amazement and I settle down next to them. There are people crowded around the manger and all through the cramped cave and outside. They are smiling and dancing and shouting Hallelujah.

I smile and whisper beneath the din "It's O'Connor's 'Revelation'!" Mary looks at me quizzically. Joseph says, "Who?" "Mary Flannery O'Connor...she is one of my favorite writers. She wrote short stories and one of her best, and my personal favorite, is called "Revelation'" Joseph looks interested so I continue.

"It's about a very self righteous woman who thinks that she is better than most people because of her own efforts. She does good things, goes to church, is kind to the workers on her farm, prays daily, believes on Jes...believes in the Savior, (realizing Mary and Joseph at this moment have no idea what Jesus is going to end up doing) and considers herself a good candidate for grace. The truth is she has never experienced real grace."

Joseph and Mary seem baffled with the word "grace", and I have to remember that at this moment in history the grace of Jesus is an unknown. They don't even know why He came exactly. I try to alter my explanation;

"There are people who try to serve God in their own power. They have received the gift of the savior but they still think there is something to add to it. Good deeds, strict rules...they don't understand that the gift begins and ends with receiving it. Whatever else we do in our lives is just done by surrender to God's use. These folks you see here...they were considered 'unacceptable' to those around them. They are sinners, uneducated, people of bad reputation, poor, vagabonds, people who accepted the Christ and still wrestled with problems all their lives. The people, who worked so hard to attain what was given for free, really don't like these people and they really can't understand that your baby would receive their visit."

With that explanation in mind, Joseph and Mary watch...wide-eyed at times, the procession of dirty, unwashed, uneducated people. They come with broad smiles because they have already received and they are just coming to say thanks.

Like O'Connor said, they have also washed their robes in the Blood and it has made them just as clean as the pious judges who wish these people were not here. Once in a while there is a recognizable face...Mary, the Magdalene...the woman at the well...the thief on the cross...Rock Hudson, who made a deathbed confession of Christ before his then-scandalous death. Most are unnamed and unrecognized. Men and women and children from third world countries who live and die in poverty and squalor, defying the word-faith charlatans' theology.

There are murderers like Andre Deputy and Susan Atkins. Con men and Crusaders, hookers and bartenders. All have traded their guilt and sin for the wondrous love of the tiny baby.

They have been forgiven much so they love Him much. They judge no one because they lived under judgment all their lives. They are the happiest to be here because so many of His "followers" said they'd never make it.

I am most comfortable amongst these folks. They are not the type to judge my actions one at a time or decide how I should be handling my challenges. They are happy to be here at the stable...which has become a marina of sorts...for a multitude of shipwrecks.

December 19

Agnes

I am sitting in the corner near a small fire that Joseph has built. Mary is asleep on the other side of the cave and Joseph is next to her, placing his coat over her against the cold. I am barely aware of much else...this has been such a different experience already.

I try to take in all that I have seen and felt. I realize I have gotten lost in thought when I see in the shadows a dark complected woman crawling through the cave door. She hesitates at the threshold, but not because she is unsure of her destination or her welcome. No, she seems to know exactly where she is and that she is free to be here.

There is something else present in her long pause at the entrance. Something that speaks of devotion...of hallowedness and respect. For whatever reason, this woman knows the value of this place and she is considering every step inside this dank, musty hovel as holy ground.

She looks at Joseph a long time with a smile. She sees the sleeping young Mary and tears well instantly in her deep dark eyes. She pauses here with a warm loving smile on her lips. Then she slowly turns her gaze toward the manger and the sleeping baby.

Crawling without hesitation through the muddy straw, she comes to the side of the feed trough where Jesus lay sleeping. There is a definite sense of worship in her every move. She knows who this child really is.

Without even a hint of doubt as to the permissibility, the woman reaches into the manger and lifts Jesus gently to her chest. Her tears tell of devotion, her lip is quivering and her hands tremble. I can tell that she is doing all she can to control her emotions just enough to maintain composure. It is a battle she is slowly losing.

I wonder if the baby senses this because in an instant he looks at the woman and smiles and coos, as if to let her know he is comfortable with her and it is okay for her to be holding him. She smiles and does not even bother hiding her emotions or her tears.

Speaking to him in a language I don't recognize immediately, (but would later realize was Albanian) she dotes on the newborn son of God as if he were her own. She speaks to him of love and affection and the many children she has touched in her lifetime.

"There were so many...so many my Lord. Always we made room but always there were more. Some of them were so sick...so very sick..." Her voice trails off and her shoulders heave beneath the blue and white robes she is wearing. When she can speak again, she whispers to Jesus..."Every child...every time I touched one of them...I was touching you, in my heart. All the love I have held for you in my lifetime I tried to pour out on them instead. I hope and I pray I made you happy and served you well."

Jesus smiles a soft smile and his eyes open for just a brief moment. Little spit bubbles form in the corner of his mouth and this makes the woman laugh softly. She begins singing to him in Albanian, a song of worship and loving affection. She is rocking gently back and forth and singing this song to her Savior...and I am watching mystified.

Her eyes close and she begins speaking names in the song...names I do not know in a language I do not grasp. But the names seem to be painful to remember because she is weeping as she sings and there is a hint of hurt in her voice. Then she speaks to Jesus, "so many...so so many. So many were sick and no one would touch them and love them. So many were alone as they died and we tried...dearest Jesus how we tried to make them feel your love in their final hours. So many children like you who were orphans almost at birth. So many who would grow up without parents...or not grow up at all. In every case we tried to love them as if we were loving you."

I watch this exchange for almost an hour. Nobody is stirring in the cave. Mary has been asleep for longer than any other time since Jesus' birth earlier in the evening. The woman has kept Him quite occupied and quite happy during her extended visit. Mary would be appreciative, were she awake.

The woman is quiet now...rocking slowly on her knees with Jesus in her arms. She has practically bathed his tiny face with her tears and she has wiped them with her headscarf. Jesus never noticed...or at least didn't mind. He has been asleep for the entire visit except for a few brief moments when He would stir.

I wonder who she is and who she was on earth. She is very pretty with her dark eastern European features and deep-set dark eyes. Her voice is dusky and her smile is brilliant white. She seems well educated and well versed. I have heard her conversing in Latin tonight as well as Greek and English and her native Albanian. Whoever she is, she is a wonder.

She frequently speaks of the children and adults she has helped at some point in her life. I wish I knew more because it sounds exciting and moving. It sounds like a life well spent in service of others. I watch her closely...

The woman has grown sullen now...something has pressed her thoughts in a direction she had not planned on going. Jesus has stirred ever so slightly and she is kissing his forehead. Her tears flow more freely now... "So many little ones like you who never see life. So many senseless deaths...and why? For convenience? For personal gain? To end a life before it ever really begins...how selfish and tragic".

She grows even more sorrowful now...clutching Jesus to her chest she weeps..."My Lord," she whispers "how they will mistreat you. How they will ridicule and mock and carve you. What a painful death you will die for me...and for us all" With this the woman is undone and her crying turns to a soft gentle wail. Another quarter hour goes by as she holds Jesus and ponders His fate through tears.

She senses Mary is awakening and, not wanting to reveal much about Jesus' fate to His mother, the woman regains her composure and places him gently back in the manger. She attempts to place a rosary around his tiny wrist but thinks differently of it. It makes no sense and she realizes it, but the habit makes her smile a bit. She whispers in his ear as she bends down to place him in his bed... "I have not always had the greatest faith...but I always believed in you. All I ever did...was for you and for the love of you, my Lord"

She turns to find Mary standing behind her at a distance enough to give her room. Mary extends her hands to the woman and the woman sheepishly returns the affection. Before she knows it, Mary has embraced the woman in a hug. The woman is fighting tears as best she can. Mary has no idea because she is enveloped in the older woman's robes.

Mary speaks after a long pause; her eyes are moist as she looks at the woman. "I am far from home...far from my own mother. You remind me so much of her...there is comfort in your countenance." The woman shakes visibly at these words...she cannot contain her emotions very well and Mary is puzzled that she would elicit such a response from an older woman.

Mary tells her, "Thank you for taking care of Him tonight. I was so weary and this is the most sleep I have gotten in days. I needed it. I really do miss my mother tonight...I am just a young girl and this has been frightening to me. You have helped me by being here."

The woman lowers her head in respect; she will not face Mary eye to eye. Mary places her tiny hand along the woman's cheek. The woman looks up slowly. Mary smiles and mouths the words "Thank You" silently.

There is an eternal feeling in her "thank you' that the woman picks up on immediately and she touches Mary's hand with her own. It is a moment she treasures...standing there with the mother of her Lord on the very night of His birth. A dream come true for this woman.

A lifetime of living for others, of service to the son of this precious little teenaged girl, has found its focus here tonight. God has, through whatever mystical means He has been employing here throughout this season of Advent, allowed this amazing servant of His to be here in the early hours of Jesus' life.

He has allowed her to touch Him as she had touched maybe hundreds of thousands of children during her time on earth. He has allowed her to love Him as a child for a brief time, perhaps as a reward for the lifetime she spent in loving devotion to Him.

But I only realize all of this after the final exchange between Mary and the woman. An exchange that begins as she finally turns toward the cave door and Mary calls to her, "What is your name? I never asked...how are you known?" The woman pauses and smiles and then her answer comes and catches me off guard. "I am Agnes... Agnes Gonxhe Bojaxhiu. But I am called *Teresa...of Calcutta.*"

And with that, Mother Teresa turns and leaves the tiny cave as she entered...on her knees.

December 20

Love

There have been times during the course of my advent journey when I wondered if I could handle what I was watching. Times when I could barely hide the pain that the scene was revealing. Other times I was so overjoyed with the expressions of worship and life that I thought I would burst.

One of the great truths I have learned here throughout this very mystical advent season has been the power of life. Life as God gives it. And today, behind this leather trimmed calendar door I see that expressed in the most poignant and direct way imaginable.

Kneeling at the manger is a dear friend and her husband. They are embracing as they worship the infant Savior together. There is a completion in their smiles and not a trace of sorrow or sadness can penetrate. That is no small task, because the husband, Frank, went to heaven a little over a year ago.

But here in this cave, next to this manger, he can still touch his beloved Pam. She can still feel his embrace and feel his skin and hold his hand. It's not difficult to understand really, because this is what we all say we believe, if we believe in Jesus. But the reality is that all those words about life after death and eternity and heaven…they are just words for most of our lives.

For most of our lives, we watch as someone else suffers the sadness of death. For most of our lives we see the pained looks on someone else's face. We offer the words and phrases we have been taught since Sunday School, and never even consider what it is we are really saying or whether it offers any real comfort.

But here tonight, watching Frank and Pam as they are reunited in the presences of this baby, I think I understand it better. The baby came for this moment. He came to strip death of its power and permanence in our lives. Because of the birth of this baby, death was laid waste for those who believe in him. He has rendered death and the grave powerless over us.

Frank is not "gone", he is not "dead", (although his earthly body surely is) and he isn't even that far away. Heaven is not a million miles away and there is not a great gap between our lives and the lives of those loved ones who have gone before us who have believed in this child. They are as close as a breath. That veil that tore when Jesus died was not only the veil that had previously blocked access to God for all but the high Priest. It was the veil between those in heaven and those on earth.

If the child did away with death than He did away with the separation caused by death as well. Our beloved are all around us, and each year at Christmas it seems they are closest. Each year at Christmas, this baby who defeated death brings life to our fondest memories of happy times with those we loved. They are in each Christmas stocking that we still hang on the mantle. They are in each card we send and receive, and in each Christmas ornament that we place carefully on the tree. We miss them, but we seem to feel them more closely than any other time of the year.

That is the hope I see in Pam's eyes as she and Frank embrace at the manger, in the presence of this King. The hope of this reunion being permanent one day gives Pam the strength to carry on for 364 more days each year. And the baby connects them and keeps her love not only alive, but vibrant and new. This cave and this poor baby, on this magical night all point to one great truth…that this little life was designed to give life to all those who would receive Him. Frank and Pam bear witness to that truth, because while Frank has gone to his eternal home in heaven, he is still alive and present in the presence of the baby-king, from whom death itself must flee, and this is the hope to which Pam clings.

…here at this stable where so many others have found themselves shipwrecked too.

December 21

Christmas at Home

The night sky was almost purple and the stars were about as visible as I remember ever seeing them here. Back in Tennessee, when I lived in the country I would go out on clear winter nights and I could see the Milky Way without much effort. But here, 12 miles south of Philadelphia, you don't normally see this many stars at night.

I was looking skyward for a long long time and thinking about how, when I was a boy, I would always look for the Christmas star as the Holiday drew nearer. I never understood that the star was an anomaly and that God had done that on purpose to guide folks to His son. I thought it came with the tinsel and the tree ornaments.

Tonight as I gazed skyward, from the small deck next to the apartment, I was caught up in those memories. Home was a long way away on this night. Even though I was home at the time. Since my divorce in 1999, I alternate Christmases with my daughter's mom and so I only see Morgan every other Christmas. And this was not my year with her.

Christmas rarely has felt normal for me since the divorce. I am very much a traditionalist at Christmas and being an intact family really mattered to me. It still does and I hold out hope that one day I will be part of a family again. I still have a lot of Christmas left in my soul.

This night though, I was lost in thought about this season. All that it used to mean and which of those things still remain now that adulthood has taken over and life has taken her best shot. What is it about Christmas that I miss the most? What were the things that made it such a favorite holiday?

The easy answer, I suppose, would be the Christmas presents. That's the part that every child loves, (and most adults if we're honest). But there was always so much more to this season than just unwrapping gifts on Christmas morning.

As I sat there in the little plastic chair on my rooftop deck, wrapped in a blanket against the December chill, it was that which I longed for. Those memories and that *feeling*...that thing in your heart that started feeling really great around Thanksgiving and built to a crescendo until December 25 and came in for a soft landing at New Years.

Some of the answers were easy. Christmas was the one time when there was any sort of prolonged peace in my house. Everyone got along for the entire month of December. It was about the only time we did anything as a family. We put up the tree, decorated the house. One tradition we had when I was very young was going to Philadelphia by train the day after Thanksgiving.

Every "Black Friday" my mother, my brother, my Aunt and Cousin and my grandmother would board the train in Ridley Park and ride the 15 miles or so to Suburban Station on the North side of City Hall on Broad Street. Then we'd walk down to the Wannamaker's Store on Broad and see the wonderful light display with a spine tingling narration by the great John Facenda.

It's old and outdated not but it still operates during the season and families still bring their kids there to feel the same magic we felt and our parents and grandparents before them felt.

When we were kids, there was a wonderful monorail that circled the toy department of Wannamaker's. The toy department was that big. Your parents would put you on the monorail and you would be up there at ceiling height, circling aisle after aisle of toys while they went and did some secret shopping. Then they'd get you and take you to get your picture taken with Santa and you'd walk around the toy department for hours wanting everything you saw.

We'd walk down the block to Gimbel's and see their walk-through Christmas land display and by 6PM we were exhausted and our heads were spinning from trying to process so much Christmas magic.

Sometime in early November the "Sears' Christmas Wish Book" would arrive by mail and my brother and sister and I would take turns going through it and writing our initials next to what we hoped Santa would bring us. For me it was GI Joes, slot cars, and sports equipment.

Christmas Eve would find us usually at my grandmother's house in Philadelphia. My grandfather would usually be dressed in a sweater and looking his best and smelling like Aqua Velva. My grandmother would be teary eyed when we walked in the door. She was a Christmas lover too.

In later years we moved the Christmas Eve party to our house in Wilmington. Open house, come as you are, and stay as long you want. People would come and go throughout the evening. I would usually sneak off for a few hours to visit with some other families who also had Christmas Eve parties. Christmas Eve wasn't Christmas Eve unless I saw the Winwards for a while.

There was almost a hint of sadness to the night. Deep inside I knew that in a day, or two or a week, the world would go right back to what it was for the other eleven months of the year. We wouldn't be getting along nearly as well, we'd hardly do much of anything together, and life would just roll on. But for this one night, there was a palpable magic in the air.

As I got older, got married, divorced and settled into adulthood, I found myself missing those Christmas Eve gatherings more and more. When I was introduced to most of my father's family about 4 years ago, I was invited to the Christmas Eve (festa dei sette pesci) Feast of Seven Fishes. Nobody eats for the holidays like an Italian and my family does it best.

The first one I ever attended was the best. I was sitting with cousins I had only recently met and with my Uncle Franny and it felt like I was part of something I'd been yearning for my whole life. It was as if a hole had begun to fill in my soul somewhere.

That is the yearning I felt this night. I was missing all that had gone before and all that might still be. There is something about my hometown at Christmas. Philadelphia really gets it right.

There is a wonderful tradition of music. WMMR is the leading AOR station in the city and at Christmas they really caught the spirit. I remember wonderful songs like Bowie and Bing singing "Little Drummer Boy / Peace on earth/". Or The Waitresses "Christmas Wrapping". "Run Run Rudolph" by Chuck Berry.

But I always knew it was officially Christmas when two songs played. When I first heard Bruce Springsteen's raspy intro "it's all cold down along the beach...and the winds whippin' down the boardwalk..." Nobody does "Santa Claus is Comin' to Town" like The Boss.

And the most poignant and emotional moment for me would always come when Pierre Robert, MMR's midday jock, would play the only known version of Allan Mann's amazing "Christmas on The Block". The first time he played that song and told the story of the blind couple portrayed in the lyrics, I wept openly. It moves me like nothing else. Because it so perfectly captures the truth that Christmas is what you see in your heart about the holiday…not what the world shows us in decorations or newspaper advertisements.

Memories were flooding my heart now. The houses along Boathouse Row, Christmas caroling on my street, climbing up on the rooftop with sleigh bells so Morgan would think Santa had arrived, the lights at Longwood Gardens, the massive pipe organ at Wannamaker's, cookie trays from Termini Brothers. There were things about this holiday that marked my soul and I was missing them badly.

Little things that you don't think about until you miss them and need them. The way a Salvation Army band sounds on a street corner. Or the way the bell sounds when you have dropped a few dollars in change into the kettle. The way little kids sing their songs at their Christmas Programs…off key and staccato but precious and beautiful.

For me, towering above all the Christmas memories was always one. It's that moment during "A Charlie Brown Christmas" when Charlie Brown senses he has lost his cast and they aren't listening to him as director of the Christmas Pageant and he is feeling his mounting disillusion with Christmas (ever the amazing introspective 9 year old) and he cries out in frustration "Isn't there anyone…who knows the real meaning of Christmas!?"

The answer comes from his best friend Linus. "Sure Charlie Brown" Linus says, "I can tell you the true meaning of Christmas". And then he walks to center stage asks for a spotlight, and quotes line by line the Nativity Story from Matthew. Every year that plays out on national TV and every year...even at 47...I will get tears in my eyes and I will know...Christmas has arrived on schedule. And just in time.

December 22

A Long Lost Friend

I have been sitting with Joseph and Mary for about a quarter hour. We have been discussing the events of the evening. It's a very strange conversation to have, knowing that I know more about their son then they do at this point. I try to be guarded about what I say. To be quite honest this whole series of events is confounding, and I have not even begun to try to explain what is happening to me.

Joseph and Mary are weary...I can see that in their eyes. I slip quietly over to a corner of the cave where there is a covering of shadow. I want them to have some time alone and I need some myself. Time to think and wonder about this evening's events. But I find that there will not be much time for that. Another guest has arrived.

A very beautiful woman, about the same age as me, has entered the cave very meekly. Her eyes are sullen and cast downward as she crawls in through the damp straw and mud. She barely looks up enough to even see where she is going. She pauses just inside the cave and haltingly asks; "I...came here to see Him...to see the baby. Is it...is it okay? Is he here?"

I know I recognize her voice but I cannot place her face. I realize that whoever she is, I have not seen her for a long time and we have both changed. She is carrying a blue diaper bag, the kind new moms carry. Mary has never seen something like this but I have. I can only wonder why she would bring it with her to this cave and that's when it dawns on me who this woman is. Her name is Kelly. I went to high school with her.

Kelly was a beautiful girl in high school, and she remains a beautiful adult woman now. She was always a little sad beneath her bubbly exterior and there had been rumors in the small Christian high school I attended, that Kelly had been the victim of a sexual predator for years.

When we were in our senior year, Kelly found herself pregnant and her embarrassed parents withdrew her from the school and it was said she moved to South Carolina to have her baby.

Kelly's parents were deacons in the church I grew up in and they were very devout and pious folks. Her dad had been a hard drinking and hard living businessman who had come to Jesus through a series of accidents and misfortune that left him feeling very lucky to be alive and needing a second chance.

The sad part was that he felt the need to earn it, instead of understanding that we all need a second chance and have nothing to offer God in exchange for it so we'd better just take it as we are.

Her dad and mom were "pillars in the church". Kelly and her sister never wore pants, and all their skirts went below the knee. Her brother always said "yes sir" and "no sir" and his hair was short and he was going to be a preacher...even though he had a marvelous gift for painting and was only really happy when he was creating art.

There had long been a rumor about a young deacon in the church and his near-infatuation with Kelly. But those things never happened in Independent Fundamentalist churches because the strict legalism was supposed to be the only sure-fire means of battling such horrifying temptations. Nonetheless, the rumors persisted and, looking at Kelly now, I remembered how she shrank from this man like darkness from light whenever he came near.

He had been a youth worker and so he was around us all the time...and he had a strange proclivity for over-attentiveness toward Kelly. He gave me the creeps. Maybe it was because I had a crush on her briefly in 10th grade and that made me protective, or maybe it was just the fact that a sexual predator was not talked about in the 70's, but for whatever reason I made myself stop thinking about the strange gut feeling I always got when this man came around Kelly.

Then came that morning in February of 1981, our senior year, and Kelly's empty desk in homeroom...and the whispered rumors began. Her best friend came to school with red-rimmed eyes the next day and all she would tell us was that Kelly and her family had moved away.

A month after that, word had gotten back to us that Kelly had moved to South Carolina to have a baby. 7 months later the youth worker resigned and joined the Army and nobody connected the two seemingly coincidental events.

Now here she was...45 years old and still stunning...maybe more so than she was in High school. Same dark hair, same dark eyes. She even smelled beautiful...like she always had when we were kids. But Kelly was not the same Kelly that I remembered just before she left.

She had always possessed a sad quality behind the beautiful outward veneer...but this Kelly had no veneer. This Kelly was as deeply wounded as any person I had ever seen in my life.

She wouldn't look at Joseph or at me and she barely could hold Mary's eye for more than a second or two. She kept darting her eyes left or right, or mostly just looking at the ground. Her jaw line was flexing the way a person's does when they are clenching their teeth. She looked fierce and angry, unless you looked really close...then all you saw was the sadness of a truly broken heart. A heart that had...as a means of defending itself against an unwanted intruder...stopped working at all. Kelly felt almost nothing in the deepest part of her soul.

I caught her eye for just a moment and I saw the terribly sad look of hollowness and pain. A pain that she'd buried long ago and that she had long forgotten the source of. Or at least she had tried to forget. She didn't recognize me when she glanced my way. Mary smiled meekly at her and bade her come in. "You are welcome here ma'am" Mary called sweetly.

Kelly looked almost shocked at Mary. As if a term of respect were foreign to her. I found myself looking down at the ground so as to avoid making her feel uncomfortable and too, to avoid her recognizing me, still wondering if that were possible.

Most of the evenings visitors had not even known I was there, but Kelly and I had locked eyes once already and I knew she saw me here. She paused in front of Mary and asked if she could see Jesus. Mary paused and I could detect a gasp in her voice... "How do you know His name?" Mary asked. Kelly was as puzzled as Mary, "I...don't know. I don't really know how I got here or why. I promised myself I would never mention His name or come near..." Kelly's voice trailed off as tears burned hot in her eyes.

I remembered now. I remembered Kelly's best friend coming to school a month after Kelly had left and I remember never before or since, seeing the kind of burning anger I saw flash in her eyes that day. Her name was Rhonda. Rhonda came to school on a Monday morning and had little to say. She sat at our lunch table in stone silence. One of the girls asked her about Kelly and had she heard from her. Then the snickering started...then the whispered jokes.

I was sitting at the other end of the table with two guys from the hockey team and I caught the most important...and heartbreaking...portion of the conversation. Rhonda told the one girl who was the leader of the attackers that yes...she had in fact talked to Kelly.

Rhonda said yes, Kelly was pregnant...4 and half months by this point. The girls kept up their relentless attacks and finally Rhonda jumped to her feet and threw a milk carton at the ringleader. "My friend wishes she could die!" Rhonda hissed, "Do you know what really happened...do you know who did this?"

Rhonda was almost screaming now, and tears were breaking her voice into short chunks. She paused and thought better of mentioning the man by name because at that point he was still on staff at the school.

Then Rhonda said something that tore through my 17 year old heart like a scimitar and left a raw bleeding edge to this very day. She was controlling sobs long enough to spit out; "My best friend thinks God did this to her. She thinks God allowed this because she thinks she is evil. Kelly wishes she could die and she thinks God hates her and she won't even mention His name again! She thinks her mom and dad hate her; she is convinced you all hate her, and she believes God is disgusted by her, and you are all acting like He is. You all make me sick!'

With that Rhonda ran out of the cafeteria and the next day she transferred to the public high school near my neighborhood and wouldn't talk to any of the girls from our school anymore.

I saw her at a hockey game later that winter and she said a brief hello to me. Before she left I remember grabbing her hand lightly and asking her how Kelly was doing. Rhonda broke into tears at this and she hugged me hard and said Kelly had lost her baby that week.

I was 17, so I didn't understand what that did to a girl and I thought maybe it was a good thing. And like an impulsive 17 year old boy I said so, "Well maybe that's for the best, right Rhonda? I mean now she can get on with her life" Rhonda must have been more mature for her age than any other girl I knew because she didn't explode at me.

Maybe she remembered the crush I had on Kelly in 10th grade or the fact that Kelly and I remained friends even though she didn't return my affections and she knew I would never say something hurtful. Before she left the hockey rink, I whispered to her "Tell Kelly I miss her...okay?" Rhonda was crying and I was looking for a door so she wouldn't see me cry in case the tears I was squashing down inside my soul managed to break free.

Now here she was, 30-some years later. I knew it was her but I was not sure she recognized me. She was whispering to Mary and she was moving so slowly towards the manger...as if she felt some sort of repellant force and was working against it. She seemed to keep her eyes down in some effort to avoid seeing Jesus...or at least to avoid seeing Him all at once. It was if she needed to acclimate herself to his presence and just tiny glimpses were all she could handle. She was about three feet from the manger when she paused and looked at Mary.

"Did it hurt?" Kelly asked. "Giving birth...did it hurt?" Mary smiled and said "Yes! Oh my yes! And it seemed like it would go on forever but once he was born, the pain seemed to vanish and I was so happy..." Mary was interrupted by the sobs emanating from Kelly's broken heart. She was already on her knees, out of necessity from the low height of the cave ceiling. But now she had fallen forward almost on her face and the quiet sobs had begun.

I wanted to rush to Kelly's side. She had been my friend all those years ago and she was so broken and so hurting tonight. But I hesitated, knowing that what she really needed...*all* she really needed was only three feet from her, cooing quietly in a wooden feed trough. Mary comforted her wonderfully and in a few moments Kelly was regaining her composure enough to speak again.

"I was carrying a son once" Kelly said, "But I..." there was a long long pause here, as if Kelly was choosing words that Mary would understand given the differences of time and culture. "...I lost him" Kelly whispered.

Mary looked baffled, "He was stillborn?" She asked. At this Kelly was wracked by a new wave of sobs. She could not raise her head to look at Mary. Mary tried to comfort her. "But that happens a lot, Miss" Mary whispered. "There was surely nothing you could do. You mustn't blame yourself" This elicited a new wave of pain and sorrow from Kelly. The sobs were almost shrieks now and under it all I heard her saying a name occasionally. "Taylor" she would whisper between sobs. "Taylor".

After a few moments Kelly was laying on the muddy straw right next to the manger. She rose to her knees and with her face in her hands in a position of uneasy worship for the baby in the manger. Mary stroked her hair for a minute and then I saw a look come over her face as if she had heard a voice. Mary glanced slightly upward and then looked at me puzzled. She came over to where I was sitting near Joseph.

"You know this woman?" she asked me. "Yes..." I answered, "But how did you..."
Before I could finish asking her how she knew that I knew who Kelly was, Mary said "I have heard the voice of my Lord several times tonight...and just now was such a time. Go to her...she is your friend and she needs you."

I didn't even try to contest. I crawled through the damp straw to where Kelly was kneeling with her face buried in her hands and the sobs still pouring out of her soul. I sat there next to her not knowing what to do or say. For whatever reason I glanced at the baby in the feed-trough.

Jesus was crying.

He was not crying for food or for attention or to have a diaper changed. He was not crying like a baby. He was lying still in his little makeshift cradle and silent tears were building in his eyes and running down his cheeks. He made no sound at all.

I felt my hand reach for Kelly's long dark hair. I touched her so lightly that I didn't think she would feel it...I'm not sure I wanted her to. She stiffened to my touch and I heard her gasp lightly. I took a breath and worked up the nerve to say a name I hadn't said out loud in 30 years, the name I always called her... "Kell..." Kelly sat up like a shot.

That was what I called her all the time through high school. She looked at me in instant disbelief for just a brief second. "Kell...it's me...its Craig" Kelly's face grew red and she look scared for just a second. "It's okay...I've been here all night" I said to her. Kelly threw her arms around my neck and I could tell she was holding back the darkest and most painful tears. We said nothing for a long long time.

I felt Kelly stiffen and she pulled away from me. Her face turned slightly angry and under the anger...humiliation. "You were here all night? You heard my conversation with Mary?" she hissed. "Yes" I answered... "I heard enough. Kell...it doesn't matter to me. I've always hoped you were okay and I always wanted you to be happy. What brings you here?"

This was apparently the question she was answering that night. She ventured a glance toward Jesus..."I came to see Him," she whispered to me. "I haven't seen Him since I was 17...since..." Kelly broke into loud painful sobs. She buried her face in my shoulder and I hugged her as tightly as I could. "I know Kell...Rhonda told me...I know what happened...and who..."

Kelly drew back and a look of horror filled her eyes. "It's okay Kell...you were the victim. You were just a kid. It's left such a big hole..." Kelly was sobbing again but I sensed a wall had begun to crumble. My instinct told me that I was the first person from high school...from when this all happened to her...that she had seen or heard from since then. Excepting her best friend Rhonda, she had lost contact with all of us. That only built on the shame she was already carrying.

"I know you lost the baby Kell..." Kelly's jaw dropped and her eyes grew very wide and tears flowed like a river. I knew not to say a word...and inside my heart I heard a small quiet voice, telling me to just listen. Kelly cried a long time and then she looked at me with more sadness than I have ever seen in one other human. She drew a big breath and after a long pause she said "I didn't lose him Craig...I...I ended it."

This was as close as Kelly could come to saying the word "abortion". But the sting and the horror was still just as plain as if she had blurted it out. Kelly was wearing a scarlet letter in her soul and I could see it. She had long ago moved from not being able to forgive herself to plainly despising herself for this one decision she had made.

Where my tears came from was easy for me to understand, my friend was in incredible pain and not only could I see it...I felt it, to a small degree. But

Kelly could not fathom my loving response. She thought somehow that I was going to react harshly and in judgment and condemnation. She pulled away from me and grew very cold.

"Kell..." I whispered, "It's okay...people make mistakes, people in pain make even bigger mistakes. I'm still your friend." Kelly was quiet and a slight smile tried to play on her lips. "Same old Craig" she laughed softly, "seeing the best in everyone no matter what they do to you." I chuckled at that, because we'd had that discussion a long time ago. The tension had eased and Kelly was a little more comfortable.

"Kelly...why did you come here tonight? You sure didn't come to see me. I didn't know I'd be here so how would you? Why have you *really* come?" I knew the answer in my heart but I was curious what she would tell me. Kelly grew very quiet and she drew a long breath. "I came to see Him..." she whispered, "I came to see the Baby".

I smiled at this, I knew that was why she made this journey, but I wanted to know what she expected from this visit. "Rhonda told me a long time ago that you want nothing to do with God or church or religion ever again. What brings you here now?" I said to her.

"Rhonda is right...I hate God..." she hissed angrily. She made no attempt at recouping those words and she threw out more invective. "My father all but disowned me and I never heard from any of my friends from church ever again. I decided that if they all judged me then God surely had. And I was so angry at Him for letting that man..." Kelly drew a gasping breath and fought tears bravely. "Why didn't he stop that from happening? Why! Why did nobody listen and nobody believe me?"

I had no answers for Kelly's probing questions. Questions that had been asked since time began. When God could have stepped in, why didn't he? Kelly continued, "I have grown so weary of hating God, and hating all that belongs to Him. I know I can't look Him in the eye. I know I can't ever think of Him as a father. But I thought maybe if I made peace with Jesus, maybe I could make peace with my son..." Kelly broke into tears again. She wept for a few minutes and gathered her composure yet again.

"I never held him...never smelled what he smelled like. I never felt him breathe on my skin." Kelly fingered the wedding ring on her left hand. "My own husband doesn't know...my kids don't know. I have three children with my husband. He is a wonderful man and he loves me. But I can't trust this with him. I am afraid he'll leave me if he finds out"

"I don't know what I expected here tonight. I sure didn't expect to see you here, and I don't know what I want God to do here. Why am I here, Craig? Why do you think? What is happening to me?" Kelly was crying softly and I looked down into the manger again. The baby son of God...hours old...was still weeping. He had made no sound since Kelly had arrived and yet he was apparently aware of her pain. Tears rolled down his cheeks.

"Kell...you are here for Him. You need to hold the baby that you terminated. You need to hold this little baby here tonight and let Him grant you forgiveness for the baby you can no longer hold. You need to reach in and pick him up Kell. You need to *touch* Him…and let Him touch you." "I can't!" Kelly protested. "I could never…" I held Kelly's hand and told her to look at Jesus. She had been here for 20 minutes now and had yet to actually look at his face. Kelly glanced haltingly into the manger and saw the tears in the eyes of a baby Savior.

I thought she would choke. She made no sound except a gasp. "Oh God! O my God what did I ever do? What did I do?" I expected her to collapse into a heap but what happened next will remain with me for all my days. As Kelly was at her lowest point of self hatred and pain and anger, I saw the baby Jesus…mere hours old…reach his tiny hand towards her.

It was the slightest move. Kelly saw it and her mother instinct raced into gear. She glanced toward Mary and Mary nodded with a slight smile. Then Kelly reached into the manger and lifted the baby to her chest. Jesus had been crying only moments before but as soon as Kelly touched him, he began to smile, as if the very touch of this weary and broken soul had given him joy. It was as if he was absorbing her pain and that made Him happy.

Kelly burst into soft sobs as she began confessing her pain and shame and guilt. She began asking this tiny baby to forgive her…to forgive her for what she did to Taylor. At this I realized that Kelly had gone so far as to pick out a name for her baby before her embarrassed and humiliated parents had taken her to a clinic and forced her to get an abortion. Kelly hated them for that and for reminding her during the entire ordeal how "bad" she was and how this was a sin and how God punished girls who find themselves in this position.

Kelly had promised herself to never even breathe God's name again in her life, but something in her getting married and then having children would not let that spot for Him in her heart grow completely cold. Kelly longed for the God of her childhood, but she was afraid of Him and felt he was disappointed in her. For years she wrestled with coming back to Him but felt certain that he wanted nothing to do with her. Then one day she got the idea... "Maybe the baby would accept me. Maybe the baby would let me love Him again. Maybe He'd talk to his father for me."

Kelly had made her journey to this hovel this year because she was tired of running from God. She was tired of being so wounded and weary and so hurting. She knew all the verses that said God heals, God forgives, God restores. But she didn't believe Him. He was probably a father like her own father, she had reasoned. If her dad was embarrassed and humiliated, God probably was too.

But maybe the baby Jesus would be more forgiving. Maybe He would understand. So she came here hoping just to see Him. Now she was *holding* Him. "My Taylor probably smelled like you do right now...he probably felt like you do...I am so sorry...so sorry. Please forgive me please...please forgive me" Kelly whispered.

She was kissing the baby softly on his neck and cheeks and his hands. Anywhere she saw a patch of baby soft skin she kissed it. I knew in my soul that she was kissing her little son Taylor. I knew that Jesus had become that baby to her. And she needed this badly. *Jesus was smiling now…*

"Kell…" I whispered, "Look at his face!" Kelly looked at Jesus and saw a smile as big and as warm and welcoming as any human had ever had. The baby son of God was smiling at this outpouring of affection from a woman who had been afraid of Him for over 30 years. She feared the father but could not possibly fear the child. The baby had no pretense and held no judgment.

I could only think of one thing to say to my wounded friend, "Kell…I know you think the Father still is angry…" Kelly's shoulders heaved in pain and sorrow and she said nothing. "Kell if He loves His son more than we love our own children, and yet He was willing to let him suffer for you, then maybe God isn't angry with you at all. Maybe He just misses you. Maybe Him letting you touch His son…hold his Son, and love on Him…maybe that is God reaching His hand to you." Kelly smiled softly at this and returned her affections to Jesus.

Kelly whispered into the ear of the son of God, "I love you…thank you…"
She placed Jesus back into his manger crib. Turning toward me, she reached into the diaper bag and pulled out a tiny receiving blanket with a monogram "T" on the corner. It was baby blue. She carefully tucked him into his little straw bed as if he were her own child.

Maybe in some ways he was in that moment. The one act of motherhood was healing 30 years of unforgiveness and pain and shame. She pulled a brand new pacifier from the bag and Jesus took it too his mouth instantly with a tiny smile.

Kelly had come here to make peace with her baby son. A baby she had given over to the hand of death in one horrifying moment. She made peace with her baby by accepting peace from this baby. On this night they were one and the same.

Kelly stared at Jesus a long time, and a smile began to play on her face. It was a smile I had not seen in over 30 years. And a smile she had not seen since then either.

She turned, picked up the diaper bag, hugged me for a long tender moment, and she was gone.

December 23

Mary

The advent calendar is almost complete now. I think about the little open leather doors and all the incredible scenes of encounter I have looked at this month.

Opening the door for day 23 I see a young girl kneeling in the dirty straw of the cave, holding the Baby...it is Mary.

Theologians will tell us that she was probably no more than 16 when she had Jesus...maybe younger. In Hebrew culture there are no "teenage" years. You go from child to adult basically, so Mary was considered a woman. But make no mistake; a 16 year old girl is still different from a 26 year old girl.

This girl had the incredible burden of bearing the Messiah...even though she probably didn't comprehend nearly all of what was going on at the time. Angels appearing to her...virgin pregnancy...her cousin finally having a baby at an advanced age and that baby leaping in her mothers womb when he hears Mary's voice.

Joseph deciding not to stash her someplace and go on without her...those angels again earlier tonight and those shepherds telling her an incredible story about even more angels and a star. People worshiping this Child with all their hearts.

This was a lot for a 16 year old girl to process. Besides all this she was still a mom. She still had the mother instinct and the whole nesting thing and this cave was a disgrace. She descends from David, after all, and there were a few shepherds in her family. She knows what kind of dirty animals they are. She probably saw this place and it made her sick but she was in labor by the time they got here and she had no choice.

This wasn't her dream nursery for her firstborn...but then this was not your ordinary child. Mary is kneeling next to the manger holding her boy...

"My son...my son...there is so much I still don't understand about all of this. Your Father is God...that's what the angel told me and I have to believe it...especially now, holding you as I am, because I have a baby in my arms and still have not been with a man. When the vision first came to me I was afraid. I thought I was going mad. How can I have a baby when I am unmarried? People talked. They said mean and hurtful things under their breath, about you and about me and Joseph. Joseph is a good man and he has a good heart. He deserved better than the cloud that followed us because of this situation, but he too heard from God about you and he decided to obey. He is not your father...but he will be a good dad. I hope we will be the parents that your Father desires us to be. This is strange...I feel like you are my son in many ways but in other ways I feel like I am the child here. There is much I don't understand."

Mary rocks her son for hours...storing up the things she has seen and heard and thinking about them over and over in her heart. "Pondering" is the word the bible uses.

Shipwrecks tend to ponder when they finally find their way to this place. It is never what they expected, and He is never what they thought He'd be. He is tiny,

195

and unassuming, and it is safe to approach Him. That's never what we have in mind for the Savior of our souls.

But that is what makes Him so beckoning to us all. That was God's master plan...it starts here. We ponder how God could love us this much. We ponder how He could send His son to us, wearing our skin and dressed in our clothes and poor like most of us are.

We ponder the fact that Jesus Christ was illegitimate, by earthly standards, and people talked. He was poor, probably just to spite the word-faith charlatans who claim He was wealthy and we should be too.

He was scandalous and He didn't just enter through a side door...He burst on the scene. The scandal of a poor, homeless, illegitimate Savior ripped time in half and history divides itself cleanly along that line; "Before Christ and After Christ".

He is the centerpiece of time and the fault line of humanity. And He lays here tonight dressed in rags, in a dirty manger, in a cold dreary cave, with a teen-aged mom and barely a soul noticing. He causes shipwrecks ...this scandalous little boy. His unseemly entrance and his meager birthplace are great rocks against which even the mighty find themselves dashed.

He is not at all what we expected...but He is all we hoped he'd be. The shipwrecked find this comforting
...and we ponder it all year long.

December 24

Why Have You Come?

It is December 24th. Christmas Eve. If you have read all the way through this book since December first, then you know the mystery by now.

Somehow, through some the plan of God alone, we have been witness, you and I, to 23 differing characters in a head-on collision with the infant baby son of God. Some of them were easy to watch, because they were people who had walked with this infant-King all their lives and were here to simply celebrate and worship and give Him their love and thanks.

Others were painful, like the wandering lost outside the cave who could not find their way to this child and who desperately need to be lead here before it is too late. Some were stubbornly holding on to their own beliefs that they had their lives figured out and they didn't need to kneel in the muddy straw and let this baby touch them.

For some it was too late, like those denied access outside the cave because they had failed to recognize this child in their time on earth and now they sought a second audience that they would never receive, but would pursue throughout eternity.

For some, like me and my friend Kelly, and others, this night represented something new and different. We are those who have known this baby but who had fallen victim to the failed teaching of strict legalists and we had grown fearful of this child's Father. God knew this and allowed Himself to come to us in the form of His beautiful little son Jesus, a baby we could touch and hold and coddle and comfort. A baby who would do in our hearts what all babies do...make us smile and tear down our walls.

For me and my friend Kelly he represented a bridge between the image we had of God our Father and the real Father that God is. Jesus the infant God called to me from my fear and self-loathing and self-punishment, and He said, "I love you so much, that I decided to come as a baby. Nobody is afraid of a baby. Come and touch me...come and hold me and let me touch you. I have missed you and I want you to come home. Let's start the journey here in this cave…come and hold me, I love you"

His call went out as he walked this earth; "Come and be my friend, all you who are so very tired from working so hard and carrying such heavy burdens, because I will give you rest. The work I do is easy and the burden I bear is light. Put down the heavy suitcase that you keep shifting from one hand to the other…it's too heavy. Put it down and hold me instead……I'm just a baby…"

For others…like Andre Deputy, this baby meant the final step of restoration and redemption, as he found the very people whose lives he had ended had come to worship this child with him. Andre, Bayard and Alberta Smith, his victims, and the infant Jesus all in the same frame of time. That can only happen through a God who chooses to forgive what others cannot even choose to stop whispering about. Only a baby could reduce a murderer to tears of repentance, change his life forever, impact an entire prison, and then reunite him with his victims in worship…only *this* baby could do that.

Only this child could so impact a Roman soldier that he would leave his post, drop his armor and risk his own life just to say thank you and to worship the God who He watched give over his son to death on that terrible Friday afternoon. Only this baby could move that gruff and gritty man to tears of joy and redemption and only the innocence of that baby could remove bloodstains of guilt that no soap on earth could wash.

A baby is the only person who could have filled the tremendous empty hole in the soul of my friend Kelly, and who could have offered her forgiveness and peace for one horrifying decision that was forced on her. Only this child could begin the journey of redemption and restoration and forgiveness. Only this child could convince her that His Father was not angry with her...but that He loved her so much that he took on a form she could never fear and could not resist.

Only a baby can remove all the man-made falsehoods regarding God and anger, and judgment, and punishment. Only a baby can teach us what God's grace is really like, how far it would reach to rescue us, and how much God longs to touch us. Only a baby can be touched by *anyone* without fear or regret. Babies have no memories. Babies don't care anything at all about our failures or shortcomings. Babies just want to give and receive love.

It is the final night of Advent. Tomorrow we begin the celebration of Epiphany ...Christ's arrival. But tonight...tonight is the last night of His coming. And He has come here to this cave, this hovel of rock and straw and mud, for you. He chose this method, this place, these surroundings, and this moment...because of you.

Everything in the plan of redemption points to this moment in time...and to this place where nobody would ever think to look for a Savior. That was His plan. He didn't want you intimidated or frightened. He didn't want you to come into a throne room, or a courtroom for your first encounter...or first encounter in a long long time...with God in human form. He wanted to make this as easy as it could be. So easy you might not even realize at first that this was God Himself.

He wanted you at ease, comfortable, free from all the things you *thought you knew* about Him, and free to just feel free to touch Him. Because babies are at their best when we touch and hold them…because then they can touch our souls in return. You already know He would die for you…everyone knows that, and if you are here at this manger tonight you have at least some working knowledge of why He came.

But perhaps the only thing more amazing than Him dying for you…is that He would come for you in the first place. He traded a kingdom for this place. He left Heaven for this cave, this manger, this poverty. Why? Because this place…*this is where you were.* You, and I, and all of us have long ago lost our way to Him. Some of us have never experienced Him before and we don't know how to get here…or what to do with Him once we realize can hold Him.

Others of us…like me…grew up with His story on our lips. But somewhere over the years, we fell down, got dirty, worked up a whole history of our very own, became ashamed of what we'd done and who we became, and we forgot that this baby ever loved us. Somehow we thought that this tiny baby, this precious son of God, ever cared about the stupid things we do to ourselves as we stumble through this life.

Somehow we decided that an infant baby can be harsh, that He can judge, that He can refuse our overtures of love, that he can *reject us.* It's preposterous but we fall for it all the time.

201

"Jesus could never forgive this..." we tell ourselves. "Jesus would never take me back after I did..." The truth is that perhaps the only thing that would make this child cry, is us staying away from Him because we think things like that.

David was an adulterer and a murderer...and God said he was "the apple of my eye" and referred to Him as "A man after my own heart". I don't know what sin you might be lugging into this cave tonight but this tiny baby has already loved a murdering adulterer so much that he used cute little terms of affection. I am sure I speak for Jesus when I tell you... "Come on, He doesn't care what you've done".

Does He just ignore sin? Does sin not even matter? No of course not. But God understands that the real punishment for our sin is the distance it creates between Him and us. He has no desire to add anything to that. Like the father of the prodigal son, He stands ready each day, looking for the slightest sign of your silhouette on the horizon, ready to run and bring you home. Just like that father did, there are no words of anger, no mocking ridicule, no rubbing your nose in the theological do-do you have stepped in.

No, there are only tears of joy from a Father who has missed you so very very much and who long ago forgot what it was you even did to drift away. He only noticed that you weren't there, not *why* you weren't there. What you did was laid on Jesus' back at Calvary. Even what you did after you became His child. All He knows is that you've been gone a long time and He wants you home.

So now you are here, on Christmas Eve, face to face with the infant Man of No Reputation. The baby-King is reaching a tiny hand out to you and he is wanting to be held...*in your arms!*

Like Andre Deputy, maybe you have a gift fashioned from the remnants of your failed life. Like my friend Kelly, maybe you need to bring something intended for someone else and let this child comfort raw and aching wounds. Like the Roman soldier, maybe you need to finally be washed clean. Like me...maybe you need to see how the Father really feels about you, *by feeling how the Son feels in your arms.*

Whatever it is you need from this moment...you are here. This is your head-on-collision with God in the flesh. You are caught off-guard for a reason. Because reasoning and intellect have no bearing to a baby just hours old. You don't need to outwit Him, out think Him, or out-maneuver Him. You just need to reach down into the little feed trough, touch the baby Jesus...and be touched.

...and join the shipwrecked at the stable, and those who have been changed forever by a tiny baby, in a dirty cave, in the city of the King.

"...and redemption rips across the surface of time...in the cry of a tiny babe"

A Word After

Well…Wick was right. This was no ordinary Advent calender, and that made this no ordinary Advent season.

I had my "head-on-collision" with Jesus like I'd needed and wanted.

I still can't explain what happened or how I wound up participating in those scenes or where they were playing out. I think maybe I had dreamed most of them, but then they were so vivid and so emotional. I still can't explain it.

I do know that the one recurring theme in each scene was the baby Jesus. As he is the recurring theme to our Christmas celebrations whether we realize it or not. The baby changed every life He touched, and He did it in such an unassuming fashion.

In all the scenes and all the interactions I never once saw anyone intimidated by Him. Those who entered the cave with fear in their hearts, left with love overflowing and the unmistakeable imprint of the Son of God on their souls. He changes people. That's what He does.

I felt so many times as I watched the scenes unfolding, exactly what I felt the night my daughter was born; wonder, awe, love, and the sense that life was starting over for me. That's also what He does. He brings life and He gives fresh starts.

Next year, I hope you'll remember this story and these images and I hope you'll carry Christmas more deeply than ever before in your heart and soul.

And if you ever need a boost, make a right down a small alley off Arch Street in Philadelphia and look for the man with the funny name speaking bad Chinese and smiling all the while.

That's my friend Wick, and I will see him next week, when I return the very special advent calender in hopes that next year it touches someone else as it has me. "He is amongst us…"

About the Author

Craig Daliessio is a Philadelphia native, now residing in Nashville, Tennessee. He is an alumnus of Liberty University, where he played men's ice hockey for two seasons and majored in Pre Med Biology.

He is currently enrolled again at L.U. pursuing a bachelors in religion. He is daddy to one wonderful 12 year old daughter, Morgan.

He has authored 3 other books;

"Sometimes Daddies Cry" an insightful view into the life of a divorced dad.

"Nowhere to Lay My Head" Craig's chronicle of his 6 month experience living homeless in 2008 after his career as a mortgage banker was lost during the banking downturn.

"Harry Kalas Saved My Life!" His wonderful book of insight and wisdom gleaned from those darkest days when his life was so upheaved.

Additionally, Craig authors three blogs; "Sometimes Daddies Cry: a divorced dad's forum" (the number one search result for divorced dads forum)

"Ice Shavings and Shinny" his general topics blog

And "Harry Kalas Saved My Life" his blog about life impact and keeping High Hopes.

He is still actively playing ice hockey, enjoying Dunkin Donuts coffee and writing songs.

He is a sought after speaker for churches, youth groups, and businesses. He can be reached at:

craigd2599@yahoo.com